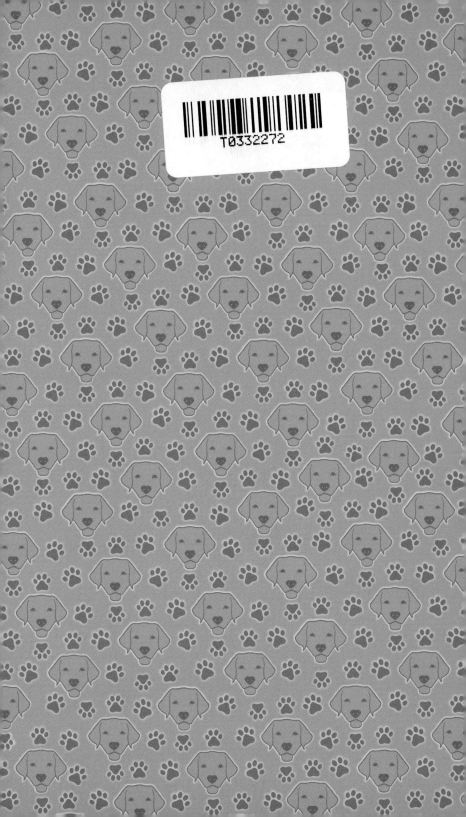

Ghost Dog

a novel

Bob Weis

Illustrations by George Scribner

Cover design by John Beach Design

Interior design & layout by Nancy Levey-Bossert

Illustrations by George Scribner

Edited by Michele Orwin
Copy Edited by Diane Hodges

Set in Ravenscroft, Epicursive Script, and Minion 3 used courtesy of Adobe Typekit, New Press Eroded by Galdino Otten

Printed in Korea

First Edition: September 2024

Hard Cover ISBN: 9798987058923

Library of Congress Control Number: 202395225

visit theoldmillpress.com

To my next generation of storytellers,
Isabella, Gabriel, and Stephen,
you all inspire me.

Table of Contents

Chapter 1 – A Mysterious Recording 7

Chapter 2 – A Bad Day 13

Chapter 3 – An Unplanned Visit 23

Chapter 4 – Welcome, Foolish Mortals 35

Chapter 5 – Cul-De-Sac 47

Chapter 6 – Up to No Good 79

Chapter 7 – A New Day 93

Chapter 8 – A Secret Shared 105

Chapter 9 – The Search for Answers 127

Chapter 10 – The Inner Workings of WED 141

Chapter 11 – Sous-Chefs 155

Chapter 12 – Back to School 173

Chapter 13 – A Magical Evening 185

Chapter 14 – Grimsley Comes Clean 203

Chapter 15 – Road to New Orleans............................. 211

Chapter 16 – The Storm.. 235

Chapter 17 – The Beauregard House............................ 255

Chapter 18 – A Little Surprise................................ 271

Chapter 1

A Mysterious Recording

It was a beautiful 1969 evening in Burbank, California. The sun was setting over the Disney Studios. Animators were finishing their day and jumping into their stylish cars. They lined up to exit the parking lot, passing under a movie billboard for *Blackbeard's Ghost.*

In the sound department, three men were working late. A voice actor settled into a chair inside a padded recording booth. He scanned a script on the table in front of him, emptied a sugar packet into his hot tea, stirred it, and took a sip.

A Mysterious Recording

"Grimsley, I assume you wrote this. You want it scary scary or funny scary?" A technician gave him a signal as a red light started blinking.

"Let's try medium scary," Mr. Grimsley, a gray, dour-looking gentleman, responded through the intercom.

"Medium scary, it is." The actor leaned into the microphone, took a deep breath, and started reading.

"When hinges creak in doorless chambers, and strange, frightening sounds echo through the halls. Whenever candle lights flicker, where the air is deathly still, that is the time when ghosts are present, practicing their terror with ghoulish delight."

Mr. Grimsley cut in. "It sounds like you're reading, Paul."

Paul, the actor, looked exasperated. "I am reading, Grimsley!"

"Well," Grimsley said, "take your time and have some fun with it."

Music to my ears, thought Paul. "How many seconds do I have?"

Grimsley looked over the pages in front of him and conferred with the recording technician. "Oh, I'd say you've got some flexibility. Let's try it."

"When hinges creak in doorless chambers, and strange and frightening sounds echo through..." Paul stopped, hearing some kind of vibration. "Anybody know what that noise is?"

The technician looked around. "Big truck going by?"

Grimsley looked unsettled. "Earthquake?"

The teacup shook on the saucer, and the spoon rattled in the cup. The small white lightbulb above him swung across the booth and shattered.

They all took cover for a few seconds until the deep rumble subsided.

"You okay in there, Paul?"

Paul set himself back securely on his chair. "I'm good, but I lost my light." He shook the lightbulb shards off the script. "Anybody got a flashlight?"

The technician raided a Foley cabinet and found a candle lantern, tarnished green from years of neglect. He handed it to Paul. "Will this work?"

Paul struck a match. "Anything to get going. Might even set the mood."

Everyone settled and got quiet.

"When hinges creak in doorless chambers, and strange and frightening sounds echo through the halls..." This time Paul became very animated, his voice deep and foreboding. "...

Whenever candle lights flicker, where the air is deathly still..."

The rumbling returned, and the room shook again, but Paul didn't notice; his eyes were staring into the distance as if he were in a trance. The candle lantern shook, making waves of strange shadows across the booth. "...That is the time when ghosts are present, practicing their terror with ghoulish delight!" Paul conjured up the deepest, scariest, most evil laugh. The room shook violently as he laughed. His teacup shook, the spoon inside it rattled violently until it broke the cup, spilling tea all over his script.

A sudden wisp of air blew the candle out.

Chapter 2

A Bad Day

Herbert looked out at the morning from the window of his school bus. His dog wasn't waiting at the end of the driveway like he always was, and he knew the dog wouldn't be waiting there when he came home.

"I'm sorry your dog died, Herbert." Kasey was just one of the annoying people in Herbert's school day. It had taken her barely a second to claim the empty seat next to Herbert, and she planned on getting right to work on his healing process.

"It's okay." He kept his eyes focused out the window, hoping to end the conversation right there.

"It's certainly not okay, Herbert." Kasey wasn't going to let her chance to help Herbert deal with his grief slip away that easily. "Besides me, Napoleon was your best friend. We're not children anymore, Herbie. We're almost twelve, and twelve years old is practically an adult. These are adult emotions, and it's likely that you will need to be in therapy for a long time. I can't even imagine how long. But the whole time, I am going to be here for you."

Herbert looked at the normal morning drive through newly built tract houses and cul-de-sacs. Everyone had the same house, the same kind of tree in the front yard. Parents greeted each other as they jogged or walked their uniformed kindergartners to class. No one seemed to have a dog that had just died, a best friend lost forever. Life just went on like nothing had happened.

Thanks to Kasey, everyone on the bus soon knew that Napoleon, Herbert's loyal dog, a mutt of unknown breed, had, with the help of a veterinarian, slipped the surly bonds of Earth. Herbert's hopes of getting through the school day without a lot of notice were ruined. Being noticed was something Herbert avoided, almost as much as he avoided

Kasey, and that was hard enough with her living next door. Standing out, Herbert thought, when you're in middle school, was never the smartest thing.

The day wore on, and Herbert tried to keep his mind focused on his classes. He tried not to notice when "Truck" Manning, the biggest jerk in school, at least as far as Herbert could tell, made dog *woof -woof* and whimpering sounds as Herbert walked through the quad after the break. *Woof-woof? What an original dipstick Truck is,* thought Herbert. *How do you make fun of anyone when you have a name like Truck?*

The only thing Herbert hated more than Truck's harassment, or Kasey's unsolicited advice, or knowing that his beloved Napoleon was in so-called doggie heaven, which he didn't really believe, was third period. For Herbert, no other class represented the evil, the abject stupidity, the complete utter lack of social relevance more than basketball. The practice sessions he actually tolerated. It felt good to jump rope, do the drills, and run to the basket. He just hated the games. He hated the ugly, yellow and green polyester sleeveless jersey. His body image was of a strong almost-twelve-year-old, but the mirror didn't lie—the jersey perfectly accentuated his scrawny upper body. He hated the endless discussion of technique and the arguments about technical fouls. But mostly, he hated being the last one picked. He hated being the *okay, somebody has to take him* guy. He wished he could just be the chameleon he won last year at the fair, turn the color of the wooden bleachers, and disappear.

Today, Coach Dale tried to preempt the situation by doing a simple odd-even count out. But after five players and two subs were selected for each side, Herbert was still player fifteen. It landed on Truck to end the standoff, suggesting that it didn't matter which team Herbert joined since he'd just sit on the bench, drop the ball, or get injured anyway.

But Coach Dale insisted Herbert be given a shot, even if he didn't want one. "Come on, guys, he's had a loss."

Coach Dale played him, and that gave Truck full license to foul him. Foul him. And foul him again. As dirt stupid as Truck seemed, he knew when he could count on Coach Dale looking away long enough so he wouldn't get caught. But the fourth foul was too much. Herbert laid into Truck's dead-weight body like a jackhammer against the front grill of a '65 Ford pickup. There is a long-standing medical argument about what bleeds more, a cut on the face or a punch square to the nose. In Truck's case, it was impossible to tell the difference.

Herbert knew his dad, Jack, was a little different.

He was tall, wore a ponytail, and as an architect, valued his creative freedom. He just didn't mix well with people in authority. This being 1969, if you had your "studio" at home, you probably didn't like bosses of any kind and wouldn't be too happy being called into Principal Brownstein's office to discuss an uncharacteristic assault perpetrated allegedly by your son on a basketball court.

Herbert was thankful his dad tried to be polite. "What was the nature of the altercation?"

"He beat the crap out of me, for no reason!" Truck's face was pinkish from the blood being toweled off, and he had half a box of Kleenex tissues stuffed into each nostril which actually improved his voice quality.

"Maybe we just have a little misunderstanding." Herbert's mom, Mellissa, was always the thoughtful, calm one. She looked at Herbert. "I think this is the first time we've ever been in the principal's office, isn't it?" She looked around at the stark utilitarian office furniture. "I like the way you've decorated it."

Early prison, thought Herbert, critiquing the design.

Miss Brownstein smiled. "I guess this is the first time we've seen you in here, Herbert, although Truck, we certainly see you here quite often."

"We had a loss in the family this weekend," Mellissa let slip quietly, with a deep sigh.

"His dog ate it, popped by the vet!" Truck added a *pop* sound to his pantomimed needle motion, closed his eyes, stuck his tongue out, and played dead, showing off his characteristic sensitivity.

The principal took Truck firmly by the arm to the only office more forbidding than her office, the torture chamber, the inner sanctum, a place you could be expelled from or just disappear from the Earth altogether, the vice-principal's office, and shut the door.

Having dispatched with Truck, she returned to her office, pulled her chair around, and sat beside Herbert. "I'm sorry, Herbert. Our pets are our friends, they're family. What was his name?"

"Napoleon."

"That's original. You must like history?"

"Napoleon liked history too; I swear sometimes I thought he was reading my textbook along with me. I don't think he could really understand the words, but he thought pictures were pretty cool."

The principal sighed. "I lost my dog after a very long time, but I just kept telling myself..."

"They're in a better place, I know," Herbert said, annoyed. "I keep hearing about this better place they're so happy to be in!"

"Don't you believe that for a minute, Herbert," she responded. "If Napoleon had his way, he'd still be reading with you, running in your backyard, sleeping on your bed, and eating cat poo."

Herbert's dad had a way of drifting off sometimes. He was a deep thinker, and he'd occasionally be lost in thought and forget what was going on around him. He stood at the door of the school office, checking his coat pockets. "Damn, where are my keys?"

Mellissa led them out toward the car; the engine was still running, and the door was wide open.

Herbert reached in, shut off the engine, and handed his dad the keys. "Here they are. You left it running."

"I'd never do that," said Jack as he stood there with the keys, scratching his head.

What Herbert liked most about his dad's new 1968 Ford Country Squire station wagon, besides the V-8 engine, the simulated wood siding, or even the vacuum-activated headlights, was the swing-out back door, revealing a rear-facing backseat. One could slide in there, be completely alone, and do just what Herbert planned to do, sulk.

Chapter 3

An Unplanned Visit

Herbert's dad talked above the car noise. "Don't think these guys are tough, they're not. It just masks their insecurity."

"Don't analyze him, Dad. He's just a jerk." Herbert called out, without looking forward.

"It's relative. You've got to look at the whole person."

"Okay, he's more of a lummox. I feel for him." Outside, Herbert was beginning to see motels, neon signs, and thought to himself, *where the heck are we going?*

"I say we cleanse our minds a little. We need a break," Jack called out, rounding a curve. "Napoleon is gone, there's bullies in the world, but life is still worth living!"

Herbert was getting curious, but he refused to ask, and by no means was he going to show any weakness by looking forward. He did his best to look for clues facing backward, a fast-moving cadence of asphalt sections, white stripes, and orange cones. The car suddenly screeched to a halt.

"Fifty cents, please."

Jack handed a dollar out the window like it was the entry price to heaven. "Keep the change!"

Herbert craned his neck, and there it was, the most beautiful word in the American lexicon, the clean, perfectly placed letters stood proudly, like giant tiles on a Scrabble board. A perfect merging of thrill with sophistication. DISNEYLAND, its medieval D, perfectly hand drawn by Walt himself. And if that was not enough, in unabashed Times Roman bold, with a striking orange background: PARK-HOTEL-ENTRANCE. The parked cars were aligned perfectly, like jet fighters on the deck of an aircraft carrier. An employee in a starched white uniform, with blue and yellow stripes, sternly made a driver back up, just slightly so that

his front grille wouldn't dare break the perfect line. Then it was Herbert's dad's turn; his hands gripped the padded red steering wheel, he took a deep breath, then, as directed he pressed the gas pedal ever so slightly, sliding into the perfect nine by nineteen-foot piece of blacktop, their own piece of Disneyland for the evening. With the satisfied professional salute of the parking lot attendant, Jack powered down the V-8.

It's probably worth a reminder that this is 1969. In 1969, people didn't just drop in on Disneyland, especially after a schoolyard brawl. A trip to Disneyland took planning. Debates needed to occur about which attraction would be first. Leftover tickets from previous visits to the park needed to be inventoried, especially those "D" and "C" coupons that still represented great rides to repeat. *The Magical World of Disney* show would be consulted on Sunday nights, for any clue, any nuance, any hint of some breaking news. In the old days when Walt himself was on, his very eye blinks and midwestern smile were studied lest they reveal some massive new undertaking. Now breaking news could come from anywhere, so you had to be alert.

Herbert's father designed buildings, shops, gas stations, carports, a four-story department store, and even a drive-in burger franchise whose owner paid him in coupons that kept Herbert in french fries for more than a year. Lacking an opportunity to study at l'Ecole des Beaux Arts, the Pantheon, or the Pyramids of Giza, Disneyland had become

Jack's inspiration, his muse, his design laboratory. Herbert knew his dad valued Disneyland, but it also fed his own thirst for reading and history as brought to life inside Disneyland, from the old west to the medieval castle of Neuschwanstein set amid impossibly tall alpine peaks, to the deadly coils of the Zambezi River.

Herbert was too old for his mom's cat-like saliva spit baths, but he was worried she might try anyway. Given the decorum of the Disneyland parking lot, he quickly used his sleeve to wipe off any residue of his victim's blood.

"Ties!" Mellissa called out. Dressing for Disneyland was a bit more formal in those days, and since Herbert's family often just dropped in, a couple of clip-on ties were always kept in the glove box, along with the reserve of half-used ticket books. Neat and ready, they entered the queue for the tram.

Herbert knew from experience that hardly anyone parked in walking distance to the main entrance. And why would they? Riding the tram was like getting ready to fly into space. It was as if everyone was with the astronaut crew, headed for the launchpad. The pristine, molded fiberglass vehicle gleamed as it effortlessly arced its way across the jet-black infinity of asphalt. Yellow caution lights flashed and reflected across the polish of the cars. Everyone knew the drill, the stakes of the mission, and had already trained extensively for it. And finally, the arrival announcement. "Welcome to Disneyland. Have a magical day!" As if anyone, at any time, did not.

"How do you think they shrink all those people?" Herbert's dad asked a lot of annoying questions, and now he was studying the cycle of real guests traveling up a tube, and becoming miniaturized into the mighty microscope, to be launched into Inner Space in Tomorrowland.

"It's a trick, Dad." Herbert tried to edge his father toward the line.

"Well, I know that. The question is how?"

"You're not supposed to figure it out, Dad. You need to work on your suspension of disbelief."

Jack settled into the line and tried to figure out the microscope from a distance. As they approached the load belt, he gave an insider's wink to the host. "It's a trick, right?"

Herbert made a run for it, trying to board the ride by himself.

"You boys go together." Mellissa opted to take her own pod, or "atomobile" as they called it; let father and son, she hoped, have seven and a half minutes of quality bonding time.

As they traveled into the world of the molecule and the atom, Herbert's dad sank ever deeper into his own version of the narration. He liked it more conversational than authoritative. Herbert's imagination took over, and he heard the narrator say, *Will the gentleman in car number 17, kindly shut up?*

Lacking any such intervention, Herbert had no choice but to look out at the ride and try to tune out his dad's attempts to make the commentary relevant. Luckily, his mom was ahead of them, and the teenage couple behind them were too busy making out to care what the geek ahead of them was going on and on about.

Herbert tried, as gently as he could. "Dad, we're entering the core of a molecule, could you use your inside voice?"

"10-4." Jack tried to make peace and shifted his focus to the sheer dread of their coming doom from being shrunk into microscopic mist.

"And there is the nucleus of the atom! Do I dare explore the vastness of *its* inner space? No, I dare not go on. I must return to the realm of the molecule before I go on shrinking... forever," the narrator went on, and Jack just couldn't help kvetching along with him. Herbert thought shrinking away to nothing at that moment would be a terrific idea.

"Thank God, that's over." Herbert exited and resisted Mellissa as she tried to wrap her arms around him. Jack was busy measuring himself, trying to confirm if he was indeed back to full size.

Mellissa pulled Herbert close. "You know your dad doesn't know how to say it, but this is his way. He just wants us to be happy again, as a family. You know we miss Napoleon too. Do you think you could try?"

"I'll try."

And Herbert did try, and somehow the spirit, and the magic and the comfort of family overtook him. As Herbert's dad had often repeated in his overblown analytical musings about Disneyland, "You just have to bring twenty percent, and the park will do the rest."

Herbert's tank was empty when he got there, and at last he felt himself being drawn into what could only be called fun. Despite it all he was being restored, and somehow the resilience necessary to imagine life without Napoleon seemed possible. Turns out, his dad was almost right; you don't even have to bring the twenty percent.

Recharging Herbert's batteries became easier as the

night went on. There is some prescriptive alchemy of salty buttered popcorn, running through a tree house, fighting a pirate, and making eye contact with a pretty girl your age while waiting for the parade. The submarine took Herbert to the darkest, deepest reaches of the Earth, and back. The skyway took him high above, where the people became small and were bathed in sparkles of color and light like a tapestry of the world as it should be. As someone in an old movie once said, "It doesn't take much to see that the problems of three little people don't amount to a hill of beans in this crazy world." It certainly didn't that night at Disneyland.

There is ice cream and there is an ice cream *cone,* hand-formed by a neatly groomed guy with a "Tony" name tag, whose forearms have grown out of proportion from reaching down to scoop up thick circles of the stuff. Herbert sat back on a Parisian café chair and chomped into it. The bite was so big he immediately felt himself falling uncontrollably into a brain freeze. An ice cream headache may not be serious, but when you're in it, you can't think of anything but getting out of it.

Luckily, Herbert's body's first response was to expand the blood vessels in his mouth, pushing blood into the freezing area to warm it back up. As Herbert's brain began to thaw, he felt that wonderful combination of warmth and cool creamy comfort food all at the same time, and just then he looked across the Carnation Garden's wide terrazzo dance floor to see his parents. They began to move, almost unconsciously, uncontrollably, to the piano sounds of the actual Lionel Hampton, playing right there, only a few feet from them and channeling all of his forty-year journey of jazz into that moment. It's said that parents just wish their kids could have seen them in their younger days when they were cool, too. As Herbert looked across the red and white terrazzo floor, he saw his parents do something he'd never seen before—they danced. Yuck!

"Step right this way." For a Disneyland employee, the gentlemen looked and acted a bit strange. He had makeup on his face that made him look possessed; he wore a strangely formal dark green and purple tuxedo; and he waved his hand in slow motion toward Herbert, beckoning him toward a gathering queue. "It's a preview. This is your lucky day."

Herbert realized they were being led toward the huge white house at the far end of New Orleans Square. "It's a preview." Herbie steered his distracted dad to get him moving in that direction, pulling Mellissa along with them.

Herbert knew this was no ordinary preview; this was the jackpot, the ultimate high stakes purse, the Holy Grail. A chance to be among the first to preview the most mysterious construction ever seen at Disneyland. For more than a few years it sat silent along the river, no fanfare, no activity, no explanation.

"What is it?" Mellissa thought it was getting late.

The cast member beckoned again, which set Mellissa on edge.

"It's ghosts, and lots of them."

She did her best to try to get Herbert and Jack moving in the opposite direction. "Is it scary scary, or fun scary?" She wanted some advance warning and didn't like the idea it was getting so late anyway. "Oh, Herbie, *dear*, I think it's late and this one will have to wait until next time!"

But Herbert hated being called "dear," and it didn't matter – he and his father were getting on this ride, no matter what.

Chapter 4

Welcome, Foolish Mortals

"When hinges creak in doorless chambers, and strange and frightening sounds echo through the halls. Whenever candle lights flicker, where the air is deathly still—that is the time when ghosts are present, practicing their terror with ghoulish delight!" A ghost voice echoed through the dark lobby, and conjured up the deepest, scariest, most evil laugh.

But it was too late, Herbert and his parents were inside now, and any route to exit was upstream of a lot of other visitors. Herbert felt the room begin to stretch. There was a scream, and Mellissa jumped. She held Herbert close.

"Mom, calm down! It's not real!"

They wound their way through the dark hallways, barely able to see their own shoes, trying not to knock into other adventurous human guinea pigs. At last, they reached an open area with moving ride pods, not unlike the Inner Space ride. As they started to load, Mellissa dropped her bag along the moving load belt. By the time Jack grabbed her bag, Herbert had taken advantage of the moment and managed to get into his own pod before they could get in.

"Take the next one. Have a wonderful ride," said another zombie employee, in yet another purplish green tuxedo.

"Jack, this was a stupid idea!" Mellissa was already regretting it.

"I'm fine!" Herbert's dark capsule turned toward them just long enough for him to give his mom a "don't worry" grimace.

A ghostly narrator came alive in Herbert's pod as it ascended into the darkness. "Do not pull down on the safety bar, please. I will lower it for you. And heed this warning: the spirits will materialize only if you remain quietly seated at all times."

Mellissa would have preferred to be in their own car, safely on the way home by now, instead of traveling through long hallways of strange entrapments, wilted roses left over from ancient wakes, and creepy shadows. But as they proceeded, she started to marvel at the ride. She was utterly enchanted with the dancing ghosts in the massive ballroom scene.

"This is groundbreaking, industry-shaking, game-changing," Jack started his review before the ride was even finished.

"This is a good time for you to *shut up*," Mellissa said, trying to just enjoy the moment.

Herbert, for his part, was loving this new ride without his father's commentary or his mother's coddling. And he was thinking how jealous Kasey was going to be on the bus in the morning.

"Kraa-kraa," a raven cried, as Herbert found himself turned around, on his back, floating through the mansion's attic window, and out into a massive, historically accurate graveyard.

"Where the heck are we?" Herbert just couldn't figure out how this huge ride fit into this little white house.

He found himself wishing this was all real; the ghosts just seemed like good friends, and they sure seemed like they were having a lot of fun being dead. There was so much to see, he almost didn't know where to look. He was sure Kasey wouldn't believe him until she saw it for herself.

Then, something really weird happened. Herbert couldn't tell what it was. It was not another brain freeze, but a wave of cold came over him, like his heart had just stopped pumping, leaving his arteries and veins static and exposed to the cold air blowing over him. He craned his neck trying to make eye contact with his parents. He caught a momentary glimpse of them, laughing, enjoying themselves as their pod spun around. He tried to call out, but his voice was frozen.

He felt his pod levitate free of the track, turning swiftly to point him toward a dark corner of the graveyard. He felt himself floating away from his parents, toward the sound of a drum beating, a bugle horn playing, yowling cats, croaking frogs, hooting owls, and other animals following the same chorus. As he moved ahead, he couldn't move or speak or call out, and he could barely breathe. His ears could hear everything, and his eyes could not close. Directly in front of him stood a team of ghost troubadours, all glowing, with bright red eyes, and parts of their skulls, bones and beating hearts visible through their blue transparent skins. Herbert could tell, although they were dead, and dressed in rags, they were definitely having a great time. One struggled to hold two heavy timpani drums on his back, while another pounded on them with heavy mallets. A short stocky man with a long droopy cap was blaring on a trumpet taller than he was. A thin man in a historic soldier's uniform complete with a bicorn hat and gold epaulets plucked away on the strings of a lyre. Rounding it out was a withered-looking gentleman, trying his best to blow the bagpipes. And off to the side, poised on a tree stump between two cypress trees, was something Herbert didn't expect, and could not believe he was seeing: a dog.

A howling dog. Howling to the cacophony of the band, and just as glowing, ghostly, and skeleton-like as the others. But then, the dog stopped howling, looked up, his blue eyes brightened, his mouth opened with a panting smile, and his tail began to wag. Herbert couldn't believe it; the dog was looking right at him.

All of a sudden, Herbert could move again, so he tried to lean up, instinctively reaching out for the dog.

"Hey, you!" The music stopped. *"Hé, vous, là-bas!"*

The ghost man in uniform had observed Herbert's

eye contact with his dog, and seemed, at first, well, jealous, and then quite angry. The dog barked. The troubadours all started shouting and pointing at once. The officer set aside his lyre and reached his hands up to the head of his buddy, playing the long trumpet. He turned his friend's head slightly, like a cork in a bottle, then popped it right off the trumpeter's neck. His headless body stood there holding the horn, perfectly content, as the soldier proudly admired his friend's glowing head. The head looked insanely toward Herbert and began cackling in laughter. The laughter grew more intense, and the head became engulfed in cold blue flames, the eyes shooting sparks toward Herbert. The soldier started bouncing the head on the floor like a ball.

Herbert's pod finally kicked back into gear and a voice came on. "Playful spooks have interrupted our tour. Please remain seated in your 'doom buggy.' We will proceed in just a moment."

Herbert yelled back at the voice. "Excuse me, would you mind if we proceed now? Now would be a great time to GET OUT OF HERE!"

"I agree," said the ghost voice.

The pod slammed into reverse. But the soldier ghost didn't like being ignored. He wound up and threw his friend's laughing head directly toward Herbert. The head raced forward like a meteor, laughing, and cackling all the way. As the pod was racing back, the head was flying forward, and now the dog decided to chase the head. The head finally caught up with Herbert, and with a disturbing jolt, magically passed right through him, lighting up his chest and the inside of the pod for a split second, before passing all the way through. Before Herbert could realize what was happening, the dog passed right through him in hot pursuit too.

Jack and Mellissa stepped out onto the moving exit ramp, exhilarated, and laughing. "Best ride ever, don't you think so, Herbert?"

But Herbert didn't react. He just stared straight ahead, standing still on the ramp.

Mellissa caught up with him, and he collapsed into her arms.

"Hurry back. Hurry back!" A tiny blue lady's voice faded away and reality started to return.

Jack ran up and they helped Herbert get to the top of the ramp and sat him on a bench.

"I'm never coming back here again!" Herbert struggled to get the words out.

Herbert's panic attack started to wane, as Mellissa gave Jack a serious, *I told you so* look. A graying, dour, official-looking gentleman of about sixty came walking up. Looking rather like he could have been a model for one of the ghosts, he said, in a deep authoritative voice, "Did you all enjoy the Haunted Mansion?"

Jack was enthusiastic, yet indignant. "Yeah...no... well, we have a casualty, that's for sure."

The gentleman took a look at Herbert and asked another employee to bring some water. "A little too scary, young man?"

Herbert took a breath, a sip of water, and looked around, realizing he was back in the real world, his traumatic brush with sadistic blue ghosts over. "Yeah, I guess a little. It seemed pretty real to me."

The gentleman sat down next to Herbert. "There's a lot of scary stuff here, illusions, magic tricks, but I will tell you this, nothing here is real. But your mind can make you believe anything." He motioned to the other employee who handed Herbert three tickets. "You seem like a pretty brave young man with a good imagination. I hope you'll come back again. Now that you've been through once, I got a feeling you'll have a lot more fun the second time around."

Jack eagerly pocketed the complimentary tickets.

"Here, I'm going to give you my business card. You have any questions or suggestions, just let me know, okay?"

Herbert took the card, another sip of water and thanked the gentleman, who quickly moved through a door marked CONSTRUCTION ONLY, and was gone.

"Nice guy," Herbert said.

"Glad I didn't need to get too tough with him," Jack said. "Let's call it a night..."

Herbert looked closely at the card. It was plain white

and had no Disneyland symbol or title or anything else unique about it.

A light rain patted on the rear windshield as Herbert yawned and took the last bite of his ketchup-only hot dog. Few things in this world taste as good or have the calming effect as a last-minute hot dog grabbed on the way out of Main Street, especially if you happened to land the last sale of the night. Herbert and his mom watched the neon motel signs and streetlights through the windshield wipers.

Herbert rolled the hot dog's aluminum foil wrapper into a tight ball. "I thought I saw Napoleon in there."

There are many things a parent knows ahead of anyone else, and although she already guessed why her son was upset, she was sad to confirm it. "Maybe you thought you saw Napoleon, but he's not in there." Outside, she was trying to protect her son, inside she missed the dog as much as Herbert did and wished to God, he really had seen Napoleon in there. The little girl in her felt cheated, refusing to understand why the world had to be so damn hard, and why anyone you loved had to grow old, and someday die.

"I *know* it wasn't really Napoleon, but it looked a little like him, except he was blue, glowing, you could see through him, and he had these big blue lightning flashes in his eyes."

"Well, that's awesome. But you know, our Napoleon is not there. He's in a better place."

"Why do all adults have to make up this *better place* story? You all know it's crap. Things just die, for no reason. Can't you admit the world is cruel? Do we have to make up some kind of phony better place?"

Mellissa fumed. "A better place, doggie heaven, in your heart, whatever you want to call it. One thing we know, he's not in a ride at Disneyland!"

Chapter 5

Cul-De-Sac

Herbert lived at the end of a quiet cul-de-sac with a garage just big enough for his father's Ford Country Squire, not to mention that technological innovation, the singular breakthrough that genetically linked car to home, the automatic garage door opener. With one simple click, the great wide door could be opened like magic. Well, it was supposed to, but it didn't work every time. Jack hit it again, nothing happened.

"Wait, wait." He tried another angle. Herbert had already jumped out of the car, hit a switch on the wall, and the door rumbled open.

Jack tossed the remote down. "It's electronic interference, probably those Russian satellites!"

Herbert's dad had insisted they buy the last lot on the circle, the one with the widest backyard, and Jack's chance to build a showcase house to impress his clients. He'd leveraged everything on their custom house, with its gleaming white and avocado modern kitchen, a meticulous office suite, and a place to seat his clients in leather European designer chairs, in full view of his clean, pen and ink renderings and stark white cardboard models.

And then there was that miraculous sparkling guarantor of happiness, eternal youth, and the symbol of infinite abundance—the pool. With its teak decks, the pool was surrounded by a perfect dichondra lawn and a custom barbecue.

Late that night, Herbert awoke suddenly from a deep sleep. In all great scary movies, the protagonist goes to investigate some noise when he shouldn't. But this was a cul-de-sac, after all, a dull neighborhood where nothing ever happened.

In the otherwise silent house, Herbert heard a distinct scratching. He couldn't tell where it was coming from. He dragged himself up, looked out his bedroom window, but all seemed calm and quiet. He tried to go to sleep, but he heard it again, a scratching. *Rats? A tree branch?*

He padded down the hall and looked into his parents' room. All he could hear was a chorus of two adults snoring.

In the kitchen, he heard nothing. There was no rat rummaging around in the trash, and Napoleon's old dog door was closed and locked. But then there was another sound, something alien, a squeaking or whimpering. He stepped outside, quietly holding the door from closing all the way. The back lawn was quiet, the decks were quiet. He lost the sound, completely. He stepped a little farther into the lawn and checked under the pool decks. A huge opossum jumped toward him, bared slobbery teeth, hissed, then waddled out of the yard, and over the fence.

Shaken and tired, Herbert headed back toward the house. But there was some other hissing, clicking sound. *What the heck?* He stood in the middle of the lawn, straining to hear. Squeak, click, click. The sprinklers! A heavy predawn drenching began to waft up from the sprinkler array over the dichondra. Herbert was getting soaked, and there were about four sprinkler heads going full force between him and the back door. Freezing and wet now, he crept into the garage, opened the station wagon side door, slipped in, and lay down on the seat.

He woke up a while later, shivering, his breath filled the air with frost. The sprinklers were finished. He quietly closed the car door behind him, but it stopped partway. He reached down and picked up the aluminum foil wrapper from his hot dog, blocking the door. But looking closely, it had little bites and rips all around it, like something was trying to chew its way to the center. He tried to force the door again, but an ear-piercing yip came out. He pulled the door open, and something jumped out at him. It was an explosion of teeth, claws, and limbs, like some kind of alien creature uncoiling and striking him in the face. He held his arms up to protect himself, but whatever it was mostly moved the air. It had little strength or weight and was impossible to hold on to. Suddenly, Herbert's entire view was taken up by two blue flashing eyes and the unmistakable sensation of slapping, lapping, sandpapery saliva.

Herbert knew this was either a terrible alien nightmare or the ghost dog he thought he had imagined had somehow followed him home.

As Herbert struggled to lead the glowing dog across the lawn, a curtain in the neighbor's second-floor window opened slightly, and someone peered out.

Although the fluorescent blue dog had less weight than a live one, he was still hard to hold on to, and it took some real effort to carry him across the wet lawn, and into the house. And he gave off plenty of light. As the dog sniffed

around the kitchen floor, he lit up the shiny linoleum and white enamel in a blue haze. And despite his ghostliness, he carried mud in on his paws just like any other dog. Herbert raided the towel drawer, and it took several of them to get the kitchen reasonably cleaned up and to dab the dog's ethereal feet from the real mud packed into them.

Herbert rummaged around a cabinet and pulled out a dusty ceramic dog bowl, with NAPOLEON neatly painted in block letters on the side. He filled the bowl with water, then balancing it in one hand, all the dirty towels in the other, he led the glowing blue dog down the hall into his room, and quietly shut the door. He put the bowl down and the ghostly dog started lapping up the water as any live dog would.

But since the dog was nearly transparent, Herbert watched as the water defied gravity, somehow flowing up along the dog's long tongue, down his throat, and sloshing around somewhere in the middle. A few rays of golden sunlight were just coming into the cold blue room. Herbert slid the water bowl and the dirty towels under his bed and slipped under his blanket. The ghost dog jumped up on the bed and, as any live dog would, circled around and around before coming to rest in a ball at Herbert's feet.

"This is going to be our little secret," whispered Herbert, and a moment later they were both fast asleep.

Saturday was the only day of the week that started with the smell of frying bacon, and on this Saturday, it was a little later than normal since everyone slept in from the late night before.

Since Herbert loved science, and he loved dogs too, he knew where the two came together: in a big black wet nose. He knew a dog's sense of smell is about one hundred thousand times better than a human's. They possess up to three million tiny olfactory receptors in their wet, black noses, and the part of their brain that analyzes and processes scents is, proportionally, forty times greater than their human counterparts. Though hard to measure practically, it appeared that the ghost dog despite his transition to the afterlife had retained at least some of this evolutionary advantage. The dog was the first to wake up to the smell of frying fat wafting from the kitchen, and by the time Herbert woke up, the dog was going berserk.

But Herbert had a more urgent problem. While a normal dog who drinks water before bedtime will need access to a tree the moment it wakes up, there appeared to be the same requirement for a ghost. Now Herbert had to get the whining ghost dog outside, without being found out.

His mom always made this annoying wake-up sound, drumming her fingers against Herbert's door. He waited to hear her walk down the hall and he grabbed his opportunity. He gathered up his new ectoplasmic friend and made a run for the backyard, waiting nervously while the dog took his sweet time, sniffing and moving from plant to tree and back again. Then he grabbed the dog and ran back to the kitchen before his mom returned. He made it back into his room, but the smell of bacon was too much for the dog, and he slipped out of Herbert's arms and ran straight back, front feet up on the face of the cabinet, sniffing for the source. Herbert followed the dog back to the kitchen, but it was too late, Mellissa arrived at the same time.

"I'm so glad you slept in!" The dog started jumping, trying to get to a height to see inside the frying pan. "Did you go outside?"

He realized he was tracking mud, and so was the jumping dog. He knew he was busted, but he gave it a last-ditch effort anyway. "I just got some fresh air." He realized she would never buy it. "I was thinking Napoleon was outside." That always worked, sympathy.

Mellissa stepped back to the stove, passing right through the dog. She had no reaction, except to notice more mud on the floor. "Can you go clean your slippers before you track any more mud?"

Is it possible she can't see the dog? Herbert watched, as she opened a closet, took out a mop, and started cleaning the floor. The dog naturally chased and bit at the moving mop, getting tangled up around Mellissa's feet. But she paid absolutely no attention.

It didn't occur to Herbert that maybe he'd lost his marbles, and the dog really wasn't there. All that was clear to him was his ghost dog was about to become the most wonderful secret ever.

Weekends were critical times for a self-employed dad to catch up on work. So Herbert was used to spending his Saturdays and Sundays reading, biking around, or building his own small projects, understanding his dad rarely had the goof-off time some other dads had.

"I'm worried about Herbert." Mellissa sat down across from Jack as he made slow progress on a very neat white model of a new house. He was at a critical point and didn't look up. "I think he's sleepwalking."

"Sleepwalking?"

"I think he got up in the night and thought he was going outside with Napoleon."

"That's ridiculous, I didn't hear anything."

"When I came into the kitchen this morning, it was icky," Mellissa said. "Muddy spots had been toweled up, but I could still see them. His slippers were covered with wet mud when he came in this morning. He gave me a lame excuse about going outside when he woke up."

From Herbert's bedroom, there was a sound, he was practicing his trumpet.

"That proves it. Something's wrong."

"I know, his playing is terrible." Jack was still half listening.

"He never practices without us making him."

Jack capped his glue bottle. "You're right. Something is terribly wrong."

But voluntarily practicing his trumpet was just the start. As far as his parents could tell, Herbert had, in just a couple of days, gone from being a fairly bookish, inactive kid to training for a triathlon. He was running all over the backyard, jumping, setting up obstacle courses, and knocking them down again. Even stranger, he was laughing and shouting the whole time.

"Something's snapped in him. Some kind of deep depression." Mellissa worried as they looked down from the second-floor window.

"Let's just try to act natural."

"Herbert, HERBERT!" A voice interrupted Herbert's athletic workout. He froze. But the dog took off to the side hedge, where a perfectly groomed, apricot-tinted standard poodle was peering in, furry snout stuck through the chain link. Herbert tried to stop the ghost dog, but he was already at the fence, nose to nose with the other dog, by the time he got there. "Did you get a new dog?" It was nosy Kasey. "Already?"

"No."

"Why are you running around so much? Are you training for something?" She craned her head around the hedge trying to see what was going on in the backyard. "Who's back there with you?"

"It's just a boring Saturday here, nothing happening."

The poodle was bouncing, trying to play, convinced there was another dog. She could smell it, sense it, but she couldn't see anything. She jumped repeatedly up along the fence, did a few circles around Kasey's yard, then came up to sniff again.

"You must have been around somebody's dog; Princess is a poodle but she's not stupid! I think you've got a new puppy, and you just don't want to tell me. What's a best friend for anyway?"

Herbert didn't classify Kasey as his best friend. She was the girl next door. Sometimes the girl next door was the only company around, but it was best not to get too close. Other girls at school were also starting to get more interesting, so it seemed best not to create any home court advantage. What Kasey represented right now was a security breach in the otherwise successful, dark cloud of secrecy around the ghost dog. And her dog seemed to know even more than she did.

Luckily, Mellissa called him for dinner. Kasey was left with her eyes narrowed, certain there was a new animal there somewhere, and she was determined not to be left out of the secret.

Could Herbert's mom have baked anything more dangerous to the delicate situation than a meatloaf? Ground chuck, eggs, breadcrumbs, ketchup, milk, onion, salt, and pepper, finished across the top with a thick layer of brown sugar, vinegar, and mustard? The ghost dog was sniffing madly. Jack was devouring his meatloaf when Mellissa made eye contact.

Quickly subduing his chewing, Jack set down his fork and started, awkwardly, "Your mother and I want to be emotionally available to you. We thought you might want to talk about things. We can tell you're struggling with the dog."

Herbert held on to the ghost dog like it was a boa constrictor in a pillowcase, writhing and trying desperately to jump on the table.

Mellissa stepped in with her part of the preplanned script. "Maybe we can see this as a lesson in the circle of life."

Herbert tried to carry on. "Actually, I'm a little confused about the whole better place thing and what that has to do now with this new circle of life thing."

They hadn't rehearsed that question, but Jack was determined to try to answer it anyway, "Well, things are born, they live, they die, and they go to a better place. And later, after they stay in that better place, they return to life, I mean…like a new dog we might get someday."

Mellissa jumped in. "Yes, that's the exact meaning of the circle of life, sort of." She looked at Jack, and they both looked at Herbert, hoping something had gone right.

"I feel better. I love you, Mom and Dad," Herbert offered. Jack and Mellissa were astounded at their success of their parenting. "Could I eat in my room?"

Herbert remembered a school field trip to Olvera Street to see the Día de los Muertos celebrations. The connection between food and the dead seemed to be as strong and vital as the connection between food and the living. So the idea that a ghost dog was devouring Herbert's dinner didn't seem totally unreasonable. The plate was on the floor, and when the meatloaf ran out, the dog licked up the mashed potatoes and even the frozen peas and carrots, which always tasted like bits of cardboard anyway. Herbert pulled his encyclopedia off the shelf and looked up Día de los Muertos. There was an illustration of an *alebrijes* dog, blue and purple in color and with its skeleton showing.

Could this be a relative of the ghost dog? There were lots of references to cultures that pay tribute to their dead by leaving food items for them. But there wasn't any advice for someone with a spirit dog with a living dog's appetite.

As Herbert flipped the pages, the dog was attentive, looking closely at the book, and licking his chops loudly. Herbert had many science and historical interests, he had marked them with little scraps of paper, and he spent some time showing them to the ghost dog, who between disgusting gurgling sounds, seemed genuinely fascinated. Herbert had marked dinosaur discoveries, various kinds of scientists, world geography, medieval history, and stories of great, heroic battles. One page had a sidebar, Napoleon Bonaparte loved Dachshunds! The idea that a famous general who led many into battle had room in his heart to love dogs had inspired Herbert to name his first dog Napoleon. He found another item about Pierre Augereau, one of Napoleon's trusted generals, and decided it was time the ghost dog had his own name. He tried softly calling out "Pierre," and the dog's ears perked up, so it seemed like the right fit. Herbert was just happy that whatever Pierre was, he was not a short waddling dachshund, no matter how much Napoleon Bonaparte liked them.

Having made it through the day without detection, Herbert settled in for the night with his new best friend. Pierre lay on the foot of the bed, on his back, his head tilted, his long tongue out to the side, and his legs in the air. Herbert hoped that Pierre's belly full of meatloaf and frozen vegetables would be quiet until dawn. He thought about Pierre's life: Was he hundreds of years old? A hero? A spirit animal? A noble pet? Or was he simply some magic trick gone wrong, and Herbert just hadn't figured it out yet?

Most dogs are sound sleepers. Cats are the domestic pets who get up to chase dust bunnies all night. But Pierre must have been more restless in his spiritual state, so it wasn't quite two o'clock in the morning when he became curious to see what else was around his new encampment. He hopped lightly down onto the carpet, then tried to use his big black nose to press open the door. He had so little real weight, he was making slow progress on the door. The hinges started to creak, so he decided jumping through was quieter. He stepped back, then jumped, passing right through the door and landing among sparks of blue light on the hallway carpet runner, facing toward that part of the house he had not explored.

His first stop was a beautifully appointed white

tile room, and he could see his blue reflection in the shiny walls and glossy floor. A little night-light revealed a kind of glistening white throne to one side with the seat flipped up. Inside was water, the tastiest water he had ever lapped up, and it was in great supply. He'd have to remember this spot. His drinking was interrupted when his front paws slipped off the porcelain and he found himself neck deep in the water, with his back end still out on the seat, tail wagging energetically. With quite a bit of paddling, he managed to just reverse himself, and got his head out, but his backside was now immersed in cold water. With a little more agility, he finally freed himself. He shook and, despite his airy presence, sent thousands of spatters of toilet water everywhere.

He looked up to see a roller, from which hung a slice of thin white paper, blowing from the wind of his fall. A slight movement of his paw and it waved like a little flag. He tried to bite at it, but it was so thin it tore off in his mouth, stuck to his gums, and he had a lot of licking to get the wet white paper out. He stood up and tried lightly holding the end of the roll with more tongue, less teeth, and it unrolled easily without tearing.

Like most dogs, Pierre was not very comfortable walking backward, but it was the only way he could keep his eye on the paper roll to see how long he could make it. He knew his way pretty well back down the hall to Herbert's room anyway. He managed to drag a line of paper all the way from the bathroom to Herbert's door without a single tear.

Proud of himself, he decided to continue exploring and see what other magical things might await him. The kitchen was more fun at night, since there were perfectly good, leftover food scraps in the trash can, and other morsels wrapped in aluminum foil like toys to chase around. The dog door was secured. He tried pushing on it repeatedly, and it tweaked a little, but he just couldn't get it open.

Time to try something else. He romped down the hall, past the bathroom to a new adventure, a set of glass double doors, closed but easy to float through. On the other side was a sparse white room with nice wood floors and a few white carpets. The carpets were so clean and soft, and just in time to dry off. He went down on his front paws and pushed his snout along for a while, shifting his nose from side to side and drying off completely. A big sneeze capped off the drying exercise, and a second shorter sneeze came along for good luck.

Pierre didn't know what an architect was, but the drawings on the wall looked pretty boring to him. He commented with a huge yawn.

Herbert's dad had lost his good sense and bought a pair of expensive leather and chrome visitor chairs, convinced they were essential to an architect's credibility. But this visual acuity went right over Pierre's head. In fact, the only thing that impressed him about these jumbles of bent bicycle handlebars was the apparent use of wide, stretched rawhide to hold the whole thing together. He gave the leather a lick and a few chews. It was really good. He decided to stay awhile. For a human, sitting on a designer chair takes some getting used to. It is mostly air, and you need to balance yourself on the narrow leather strips that form the only sitting surface and backrest. But to a dog, it was impossible. He leaped up, but all four of his legs went through the leather straps, leaving his upper body on the seat, and his legs dangling helplessly just above the floor. In theory, his ghost nature could have saved him from this entanglement, but he wasn't thinking clearly. He pulled up one leg, then the other, and the third would come up at the expense of the first two slipping back down. Not knowing what else to do, he settled on the pure ecstasy of chewing through the leather for a while. This worked until he tugged too hard on the strap, flipping the whole chair over and trapping him inside. His ghost nails softly skittered on the wood floor until he could free himself.

Running away from that danger, he found another double door opening, where a noise stopped him in his tracks. Some large animal was sleeping, and by the sound, it was possibly a bear or something even larger. But then Mellissa turned toward him in her sleep. He could tell she was the alpha dog of *this* household, and the other guy, although he snored the loudest, looked pretty submissive. Pierre decided the only proper thing was to quietly take the lowest position in the pack's hierarchy, so he jumped carefully up, did a few circles, and curled up at the very foot of the adults' bed. Between the soft blankets and the rhythmic snoring, he was asleep in no time.

Herbert had been happy to be the only member of the family to see Pierre all day, and he certainly took advantage of it. But when he woke up, he found himself completely in the dark. There was no glow of blue at the foot of his bed, no faint heartbeat like a candlelight. He opened the door, stepped into the hall, and found the end of a roll of toilet paper. He followed it all the way to the bathroom where in the night-light he confirmed that a ghost dog can leave as many footprints and spatter marks as a real one. He was becoming more annoyed than panicked. He reeled in all the toilet paper, then carefully cleaned the big black paw prints off the seat.

Down the hall he tiptoed into his father's office studio. All was quiet. But when he saw the expensive client chair, he heard in his mind his father's frequent order: *no one touches these chairs except clients, the leather is delicate and expensive.* And here was a chair, turned over, with canine bites in the Italian leather. Herbert righted it quietly, spit on his hand and tried to rub out the chew marks. Thankfully, they mostly showed up on the underside.

In the kitchen, the trash had been ransacked, there were a few empty food wrappers on the floor, and a foil container, mostly licked clean. He followed the sauce trail and realized the dog door had been scratched and hit from inside. *Pierre could have gone out! If he went through the fence, how would Herbert ever find him?* He quietly opened the kitchen door and ran around the backyard, looking under the decks, and checking inside the garage side door.

"What are you searching for?" Herbert froze. A light when on, and caught him, a convict in mid-escape.

"Nothing." He knew it was a worthless response and his mind was racing for the next one. Kasey, shivering in a Michael Nesmith T-shirt, leaned out of the second-floor window, wielding a giant flashlight.

"Can you put that out?"

"Not until you tell me the truth."

"What truth? Cut off that damn light."

She cut the light but that didn't keep him from seeing her piercing black eyes. "You have a new dog."

"No!"

"Cat, then."

"No cat, no dog. Nothing...alive!"

"Tell me now, or I will scream, and every light in this house will be on."

"Okay, okay. I have a dog. Sort of..."

"How does anybody have sort of a dog?"

"Can you let me go?"

"Only if you promise, I expect the complete story tomorrow. Just say you agree?"

Herbert realized he had no other options. "I agree," he sang out lightly.

"Swear it!"

"I swear, already." Herbert gave up.

"Sort of a dog, I can't wait." And she slammed the window down.

Where could Pierre be? Herbert settled back down

after checking the closet and under his bed. He heard a change in the snoring down the hall. His father must have shifted position, there were a few random snorts, and he settled back into his familiar snoring cadence. A sense of dread came over Herbert. He padded down the hallway runner as silently as he could, then saw, through the crack between the door and the carpet, the faintest line of blue light. He carefully pushed open his parents' door, and to his horror saw Pierre. Not just in their room, not just on their bed, but he had migrated, and was now sleeping between his parents, tongue out, happily absorbing their warm breath.

Mellissa stirred slightly, facing away from the danger she had no idea lay right behind her. "Herbert, what are you doing up?"

"I just needed some water." Again, with a stupid first excuse.

"Are you sick? Are you sleepwalking?"

A mother's concern could always be counted on, especially if you have a good follow-up, "I was a little scared."

She found him in the dark and hugged him.

Jack stopped snoring. "Herbert, why is there a dog in this room?"

"There's no dog, dear. Herbert was just feeling a little

scared."

"There is a dog," Jack insisted. "I know there is a dog because I can smell it, it's standing on top of me, and it's licking my face. THERE IS A DOG IN HERE!"

Mellissa reached for the light, then turned toward Jack. Jack was holding thin air, spitting off the sopping, obviously excited affection of a big but invisible dog tongue, but there was simply nothing there. Jack screamed like he hadn't screamed since he was a kid.

Cul-De-Sac

Mellissa screamed with him, certain that her husband had become possessed. The lights went on next door, and dogs barked around the neighborhood.

Herbert leaped up and was broadsided by Pierre, who he alone could see, forcing him to fall backward onto the floor. The dog ran down the hall, slid around the corner, and jumped into Herbert's bed trying to hide under a mass of blanket. Herbert jumped in and tried to smooth out the hump where the dog was hiding. Mellissa and Jack appeared in the doorway and turned on the light. Jack reached slowly toward the writhing mass and pulled the blanket up, revealing nothing. But it was a nothing that was a *something*, and that *something* had weight, because it made an impression in the mattress, and as the shape moved across the mattress, it made four canine paw impressions into the sheets. The invisible creature came up to Herbert who didn't move. And there was a licking, slurping sound. Jack and Mellissa heard it distinctly, but saw nothing, until they leaned in, looked closely at Herbert, and realized thick dog saliva was running down his face.

Mellissa had called Dr. Abara when Napoleon died, thinking they should have a family therapy session to discuss their grief openly. Now the situation had become much more urgent. The family squeezed together on a big black leather chaise lounge. On the walls were degrees in psychology, Eastern medicine, and an impressive collection of psychedelic posters featuring Jerry Garcia and the Grateful Dead. Dr. Abara's lava lamp collection was the perfect complement to the bead curtains and bamboo houseplants. Herbert set down his large backpack, with the top panel resting open.

"And just how is everyone getting along?" Dr. Abara was about seventy, but in her own words she was "as vibrant as a twenty-year-old." Her dress was batik with small animal patterns, and her wooden bead necklace rattled as she came in. "I'm so sorry to hear about Wellington."

"His name was Napoleon." Herbert was already a bit bored.

"Of course, Napoleon, another heroic name." She settled on a white chair with a spiral pad, flipped over an egg timer, and exhaled deeply. "Now, family, let your emotions flow."

Jack took a look around. "These posters are really awesome. Did you get them at a concert?"

"Actually, Dr. Abara, we've been adjusting fine to Napoleon. It seems we have this other problem now." Mellissa elbowed Jack, in *a little help here* fashion.

"I have a new dog. I think he followed me home." Herbert thought honesty might be the best way to move things along.

"A stray. How generous of you all to rescue an innocent animal."

"Actually, I think the dog is a ghost," Herbert said, trying to be clear.

"We believe the dog could be some kind of by-product of Napoleon's loss," Mellissa added.

"I'll do the diagnosing here, thank you." Dr. Abara took a deep breath. "Young man." She motioned to Herbert and made a direct line with her bony finger from where he was sitting to a spot right next to her. "Sit here," she said.

He dragged himself over, and she snuggled sickeningly close to him.

"Did Napoleon return to visit you?"

"No, it's just the ghost of some other dog. I think he came from Disneyland."

"How's school these days?"

"Just normal, I guess." The backpack sagged and fell

over, the top shifted around a little.

"Anything you worry about, at school, I mean?"

"Just an idiot who bothers me in PE, and Kasey who lives next door, but she's just annoying and kind of nosy, that's all."

"Nosy neighbors are a type unto themselves. There are entire studies written on just that syndrome."

Mellissa tried to track Herbert's eyes as he followed something around the room. "I feel that we are straying from the topic, Doctor. Can we get back to the matter of the dog?"

"What dog?"

"The ghost dog!"

"Ah yes, the *ghost* dog. Now can we continue, Herbert?" Dr. Abara focused her attention on him again. "A little more information, please. How are your classes, I mean?"

"He's doing great," Jack jumped in.

"If you'll excuse me, the question was directed to Herbert." She sang out the name Herbert, as if to put the rest of the room on notice that she asks the questions here.

"Now about those classes?"

"I like to read, I like science..."

"How's math?"

"I hate it!"

"Herbert!" Mellissa didn't like his tone.

"Ha! I hate it too! Anything else you especially like?"

"Mostly, I like history, that's why I like to read so much."

"What kind of history is your favorite?"

"All kinds, Medieval, Colonial, European. I like castles, battles, dungeons..."

"And ghosts! There's always ghosts in old castles!" She looked at Mellissa and Jack and mouthed *bingo*.

"Is it possible, Herbert, that all this reading of history, and your loss of Wellington..."

"Napoleon."

"Whatever. That this could be influencing your desire to make up a ghost dog companion?

The bamboo curtain, a Tibetan table, and the three lava lamps all shook violently. Jack reacted quickly and managed to catch all the lava lamps, but everything else went flying. Her curtain twisted into a mass of puka shells and sparkling beads. Dr. Abara froze.

"Telekinesis! In my very office!" She looked into Herbert's eyes. "Do it again!"

"Do what again?" Jack was still balancing three lava

lamps.

Dr. Abara's voice became slow and melodic, her eyes narrowed. "Telekinesis, movement, levitation of physical objects by purely mental waves." She felt Herbert's temples. "Do you feel it, Herbert, do you feel the intense power you now have?"

"I'm pretty sure the dog knocked it all over. I'm sorry, Doctor." Herbert wrenched away from her and went back to the backpack. He whistled. An invisible object made a flat trail across the shag carpet like a dog might rub its backside, the backpack's flap moved, and the bag expanded and shook for a second.

The doctor was overwhelmed. She leaned back in her chair and looked faint.

"Do you think it's a magic trick?" Mellissa asked.

Dr. Abara's tone became ominous. "Magic? My dear, magic is sometimes the only way we humans can make normal of the paranormal."

Jack set the lava lamps carefully on the desk. The egg timer dinged; the session was over. Herbert swung the heavy backpack over his shoulder.

Dr. Abara gathered them in a circle, snatched her payment check from Mellissa, and made them all join hands.

"It doesn't matter if I believe it." She looked at Jack. "Or if you believe it, or you, Mellissa. What matters is, does Herbert believe it?" She looked at Herbert and squeezed his hand. "Do you, Herbert, do you believe it?"

"He looks pretty obvious to me."

She saw them to the office door.

Mellissa needed an answer. "What do we do now?"

"That, my dear, is simple," the doctor noted. "The easiest therapy in the world!"

Herbert was already headed for the hall.

"Wherever the dog came from, return him. He certainly was in *that better place*, but now he's found your home, and he likes that even _better_! Do it quickly before it's too late."

"Return the dog, to the Haunted Mansion?"

"Certainly. You better take me with you. We'll need to seal the deal with a brief séance."

"A séance, at Disneyland?" Mellissa was beginning to regret the entire visit, not to mention the fee.

"A perfect plan, and wonderful weather this time of year. As close to midnight as we possibly can."

Chapter 6

Up to No Good

The sparkling clean, uplifting optimism that is Disneyland had somehow become foreboding. The normally friendly employees seemed to look at the group with a sense they knew they were up to no good. Mellissa did her best not to look suspicious, even though she felt very suspicious. Jack wondered if the old jail in Frontierland had space for four more convicts. Dr. Abara thought that even with a free Disneyland ticket, she should have charged them a session fee. And Herbert just wished his parents had never found out about Pierre. He and his ghost dog could have had a secret friendship, for who knows how long.

Secretly, Herbert was hoping Dr. Abara was a quack. *If I can just make them all think Pierre is gone, she'll be out of here, and I'll do a lot better job of keeping him under wraps next time.*

"Welcome to Disneyland." A friendly security host showed up, at the wrong time and took an interest in Herbert's backpack. "That's not a picnic, is it? We've got some lockers available over there."

"Picnic, oh no, we didn't come to Disneyland for a picnic, just a séance. I mean, no if we had a dog, we would have left it in the kennel. You sure like dogs here, we do too, and the hot dogs, though, I mean the ones we buy here. We never just, bring them in."

The guard might have been fine before, but now he really was intrigued. "Young man, would you mind if I take a look inside your backpack?"

"No problem, sir." Herbert loosened the buckle. Dr. Abara leaned nervously as the guard took a look. Jack started sweating, and Mellissa heard blood rushing to her ears.

Herbert decided it was best to just be cool. He was

the only one who saw the glowing mass of ghost dog launch out of the pack, just as the security host and Dr. Abara peered in. The dog flew past them and did a circle around Town Square, sniffing and wagging, until he came to a stop to relieve himself on an authentic 1920s fire hydrant, perfectly red, surrounded by a circle of freshly planted marigolds.

As if Herbert was watching in slow motion, he saw the security host and Dr. Abara's heads lean back, just as the dog jumped back in the backpack, turned tail down, and looked up panting and pleased with himself for such an efficient relief stop.

Seeing nothing, the security host waved them on. "Have a wonderful evening, folks."

The park crowds had thinned out, and those who remained were heading down Main Street toward the exits.

"Ladies and gentlemen, boys and girls, Disneyland will be closing in fifteen minutes, we hope you've enjoyed your visit..." Jack Wagner's normally friendly announcements seemed to accuse them now; they knew they were about to defy the most authoritative voice in the nation.

At an outdoor café in New Orleans Square, the jazz band packed up their instruments and scores, and folded their music stands. A custodian, dressed in bright white, mopped the terrazzo floor. Herbert moved toward the entrance to the Mansion, which seemed darker now. "Still doing previews?"

The security host in the purple and green tux looked at his watch. "Almost finished. If you hurry, you might just make the last ride."

"Come along, family, come on, son, this way... grandma!" Jack's acting was way over the top, and Dr. Abara was calculating her overtime now. They made it on the very last ride. Jack rode silently with the doctor, and Mellissa rode with Herbert. The ride was exactly as it was the first time.

As they approached the graveyard scene, Herbert motioned to the troubadours. "See, they're there, just like they were. But where's the dog? See, the dog isn't there." The music seemed to be Pierre's cue, and he struggled against the backpack. His ghost nose finally peeked out and took a few sniffs of the blue smoky air. The dog's robotic musician costars just played their parts and did nothing out of the ordinary.

"An admirable artistic effort at an operatic scale!" Dr. Abara gave the ride an enthusiastic review.

"Let's get to work," Jack said under his breath, and motioned to them all to follow. He led them up the exit ramp, but then veered off, heading through the door marked

CONSTRUCTION ONLY.

They huddled inside the door of the dark room waiting for the voices outside to fade. Jack turned on a flashlight, and Mellissa screamed. In front of them was a huge coffin, standing on end.

Jack moved the light around. "It's nothing, it's just fake. Look, it's a clock, a coffin clock, great idea!" The flashlight revealed they were hemmed in on all sides by weird props, and wooden crates with straw stuffing hanging out of them. Jack flashed the side of a large crate revealing MUSEUM OF THE WEIRD stenciled in large black letters on the side. He moved through the dark workspace, and they all followed close behind him.

"I think Pierre's got to pee again." Herbert was barely able to hold the backpack, Pierre was rustling around too much.

"He'll have to hold it," Jack said as he approached a large folding table, covered with blueprints. "Wow, here's all their designs!" He and Herbert moved in and tried to read the plans, filled with artifacts and historical details.

Dr. Abara checked her watch. "Gentlemen, gentlemen, we have a task to do."

Jack reluctantly moved the plans aside, clearing a

space in the center of the table. He moved four chairs into a tight circle.

Dr. Abara lit a small bundle of sage and waved the smoke around. Then she sat down and motioned to everyone to take their seats. "Will you all join hands, please? We are gathered here bonded to the beloved and energetic canine spiritual visitor, what's his name?"

"Pierre."

"Ah yes, Pieeeeeerre, from the long line of confidants of the great general Napoleon, whose bravery in battle..."

"Do we have to go through so much detail?" Mellissa was getting more nervous by the second. Herbert grasped her hand, and Jack set the flashlight on the table so he could hold her other hand.

"Now then, Herbert, do you want your ghost-dog-real-world transplant to return to his rightful family, and his familiar surroundings where he..." Jack's flashlight rolled off the table, hit the ground, and went out.

"Now what do we do?" Mellissa whispered, straining to see, but it was completely dark. Jack felt around trying to find the disabled flashlight.

Dr. Abara cleared her throat. "Herbert, do you agree, is your dog ready to go home?"

Herbert said sadly, "Can I say good-bye to Pierre, before I let him go?"

"Certainly, young man. I have a match, but I can't see my hands in front of my face, let alone where my bag got to." She felt around the table. Herbert opened the backpack a crack. He alone could see the slight blue glow of Pierre's eyes.

"If you need a light, I am happy to help," a resonant voice offered.

"Who was that?" Mellissa whispered.

"Wasn't me."

"Jack, stop playing."

Jack whispered, "It wasn't me."

"Then who was it?" Mellissa felt a burst of hot air.

Pierre began to bark aggressively, growling in between.

Suddenly, the entire table lit up in golden light, and standing before them, was a towering man, or a candelabra, or more accurately, half-man half-candelabra, complete with bronze metal skin, and burning candlesticks for hands.

"It's me, entirely at your service."

Someone screamed. Pierre dove out of the backpack. Herbert tried to catch him, but he slid out of his arms and made a run for it. Jack reached down and found the

flashlight, tapped it, and thankfully it lit up again. Herbert ran after Pierre, Mellissa and Dr. Abara ran in pursuit of both of them, and Jack just ran like hell, trying to keep a step ahead of the heavy footsteps of the candle man who was so close behind him he could feel spattering hot wax on his back. Jack cleared an open doorway, struggled to pull up the door stop, and slammed the door right in the candle man's burning bronze face.

Up to No Good

As Herbert struggled to follow Pierre, he realized the Haunted Mansion was designed to be seen from the ride path. In the dark, with barely any light, it was a scary and confusing maze with so many obstacles to trip over. "Pierre!"

"Herbert, Herbert! Herbie!" Jack shined his light down an endless hallway, then banged his head on a piece of glass at the end. The cut on his head bled a little bit. "These effects guys are tricky." He put his hands out in front of him, leading more carefully.

The settings glowed in the eerie green light cast by the exit signs, and an alarm bell was now ringing. Jack led them into a huge hall, shining the light up toward a chandelier, and large portraits on the wall. "It's the ballroom, but where are the dancers?" He took Mellissa's hand, bowed, and did a nice ballroom dance move in the middle of the room.

She pulled away from him. "Jack, our son is wandering around in a graveyard trying to find a dead or imaginary or whatever kind of dog. Can we take a rain check?" There was suddenly music coming from a pipe organ, and a scream coming from Dr. Abara. They raced into the dark to find the doctor had fallen into the organ, strange skulls filled its pipes, and she was entwined in a mass of spider webbing.

The old graveyard was silent. A pair of iron gates

looked so old they had rusted open, crumbled into the ground, and grass had grown up around them. Herbert moved along slowly, trying to feel his way. He tripped and fell, and looked up into the huge, panicked eyes of a man holding a shovel. He quickly turned around, looking right into the eyes of a dog. "Pierre!" He reached out, and realized this was not Pierre, the dog was frozen still. The man and the dog were merely robots. In the distance, he heard Pierre's little howl. He got back up and kept moving toward the sound.

"Where are you, Pierre?" Herbert's voice echoed across the vast hillside of gravestones. *Where the heck is he?* And then Herbert saw him, his blue glow unmistakable in the otherwise green exit light. "Pierre, get back here!" The dog didn't seem to hear him. He trotted up to his troubadour friends, stopping to sniff each foot and look up into each empty face. They were no longer glowing ghosts, with bright red eyes, but dark transparent plastic with mechanical parts inside. The guy no longer played the timpani drums, the short stocky man with a long droopy cap was no longer playing his trumpet, the soldier in the bicorne hat was frozen, his lyre standing still, and the withered-looking man's bagpipes were totally deflated.

Up to No Good

Looking sad and confused, Pierre worked his way up to where Herbert had first seen him, up to his place on the tree stump between the two cypress trees. He made a few circles and was about to sit carefully on the tree stump, when Herbert called out, "Pierre, no, don't sit there, Pierre!" The dog set himself down, looked across at Herbert with a last flash of blue light in his eyes, and went dark.

"Got ya!" Strong hands caught Herbert as he stumbled over fake rocks and props trying to get to Pierre. A circle of flashlights lit the ground as shadowy maintenance workers helped Herbert up and onto a catwalk.

"What was he talking about?"

"I have no idea."

"Some people, they just get a little bit nutty in here."

It was nearly one o'clock in the morning and considering how implausible the family's story was—*their son had just gotten lost*—the Disneyland security host was pretty darn nice. Skeptical, but professional. Herbert had some water from the water cooler, Jack got a spray of Bactine and a Band-Aid for his forehead, and Mellissa tried her best to pick cobwebs out of Dr. Abara's hair and beaded necklace.

"It's just a little adhesive sprayed through an air gun. It will wash out," the security host tried to explain.

Dr. Abara batted at the white stuff. "It's disgusting. I feel like an oversized silkworm."

A long golf cart picked them up behind the Haunted Mansion, and flashing its yellow lights raced through the park and down Main Street, into the parking lot and pulled up right in front of their car. Hard to tell who was more excited from the ride, Herbert or Jack. The security host watched as the family loaded up. He asked Jack if the bump on his head was okay. Then he came around the back door and checked on Herbert.

"It's a big place, a little scary when you get lost," he said.

Herbert gave him a funny look. "Don't I look a little old to get lost at Disneyland?"

"Yeah, so, you want to tell me what really happened?"

"There is a ghost dog in there, and he followed us home. Now he's gone back, and I guess he doesn't want to come home with me anymore."

The security host looked thoughtfully at Herbert. Anywhere else he might have considered this story made-up bunk. But at one-fifteen in the morning, in the Disneyland parking lot, somehow, he had no doubt that *Herbert* believed what he was saying was absolutely true.

Up to No Good

"We'll keep an eye out for him," he said warmly. Then he closed the back door and watched them drive away.

Chapter 7

A New Day

Herbert had once done a science project about the brain. In his research he'd learned that sleep is to the brain what a hot bath is to the body. The bad experiences we have the day before get processed at night by short-term memory banks, carefully smoothing over some of the emotions, leaving the simpler facts of the event in place, before carefully categorizing it all away in our long-term memory. *That's why teachers, doctors, and grandmas,* he wrote, *all say, "You'll feel*

better in the morning." With a good night's rest, we wake up with renewed perspective and ability and smile at ourselves, and think, "What was all that about yesterday?"

The golden rays of sunrise shone through the windows of Jack and Mellissa's bedroom, and although they were tired from the long night before, everything seemed beautiful. They couldn't wait to start their day. The memory of the night before seemed to fade into that kind of odd, even silly story that someday they'd laugh about around a holiday or anniversary table.

From down the hall, the parents heard the distinctive clearing of the spit valve on Herbert's trumpet, followed by a few dreadfully off-tune notes, confirming to them that life, if not perfect, had certainly returned to normal.

But then, Herbert's awful trumpet sound changed. It became the most magical sound imaginable.

Herbert was playing perfect jazz.

The parents ran down the hallway and threw open Herbert's bedroom door. There was their son, cowering on the bed. Next to him, a blue glowing dog, with lightning flashes in his eyes, now clearly visible to both of them. At the foot of the bed, were two human figures, also clearly visible but as transparent and blue as the dog. A short stocky man

with a long droopy cap was improvising jazz on Herbert's trumpet. A tall thin soldier in a uniform complete with a bicorne hat and gold epaulets plucked away at the strings of a lyre. When he saw the parents, the soldier reached over and pulled his friend's head right off his shoulders, and tossed it, cackling and glowing toward the dog, who caught it on his nose like a seal. Then the dog tossed the head to Mellissa, who screamed and pushed it off, sending it bouncing down the hallway, and into the kitchen, where it blasted right through the dog door, with the ghost dog in full pursuit, and Herbert, in pajamas, running right after them.

Herbert opened the garage door and jumped on his bike. A gardener trimming roses, a man in slippers picking up his paper, and a young woman polishing her VW all saw Herbert pedaling way too fast on his bicycle, carelessly weaving between sidewalk and street, and almost getting run over by Gennie Martinez' new Thunderbird as she backed blindly down her driveway, as she always did. Herbert's view was suddenly filled with chrome trim and white hard top. He banked just in time, blasted a route through two full trash cans, jumped the curb, and struggled to retain his balance. He

A New Day

looked back long enough to receive a well-deserved warning hand signal from Gennie. *Thank God, he didn't scratch her car*, Herbert thought.

As he turned back, something else filled his view and it was too late to stop. He burned rubber, spun around, hit the curb, and collided into Kasey and her dog, Princess, tangling them all up in the bike and the dog's leash. Princess saw her moment of freedom, slid out from the mess, and pulling her leash with her, took off in the direction of the ghost-dog-ghost-head-chase.

In the big park at the center of the development, Princess had made a wonderful discovery, a new friend. She bounced along, sidestepped, dared, ran, barked, and teased with another dog, happy to be free of her owner, and in a state of being that only a canine can understand. As Kasey reached the edge of the park, she thought her normally well-behaved, impeccably trained, just-shampooed poodle had gone wantonly insane. She dragged her rhinestone-studded leather leash through the muddy grass, rolled, snapped, barked, went down on her front legs, and jumped, everything she would normally do playing and flirting with another dog. Except there wasn't another dog. The park was deserted.

Herbert was out of breath as he reached the park and came up next to Kasey. All of a sudden, his urgency melted, and he just couldn't help laughing out loud. Pierre and Princess were so cute together, chasing each other across the park. "I guess they really like playing together!"

Kasey froze and looked at Herbert like he was insane. "Who is playing?"

Herbert had been so caught up in the dog's fun, he completely forgot Kasey could not see Pierre.

"You lied, Herbert. You promised to tell me, and now you're just making fun of me with some kind of trick." Kasey was really angry.

"Wait, no, it's not a trick, I promise. I can explain it to you."

Princess yipped loudly. She had been running hard, and her trailing leash had gotten stuck on a playground slide. She was pulling it but couldn't get free. Kasey and Herbert ran to try to free her, but Princess was so panicked, she snapped at them. She was coughing and hacking, trying to break free but the leash was taut, tightening around her neck.

"We've got to help her," Kasey cried.

As the leash tightened, Kasey watched in disbelief as something started to gnaw away the middle of the leash, some kind of invisible sharp force tore away at the leather until it had only one strand, and Princess was able to break free.

Jack and Mellissa pulled up, opened the car door, and Jack made a loud, authoritative whistle. Unseen by Kasey, Pierre had a little nose-to-nose moment with Princess and then took off into the car. Herbert followed him, and Jack sped away.

Kasey stood in the middle of the park, stunned, holding Princess on her torn leash in one hand, half of the frayed leash in the other, and wondering, *what the heck just happened?*

"Thank God." Jack rounded the corner toward their street.

"Herbert, are you okay?" Mellissa looked back and saw Pierre licking road burn off Herbert's cheek.

"We're okay." Herbert looked back at his mom. "Look out!" Something smashed against the windshield. It was the bluish glowing head of the ghost, eyes wide and electric, tongue sticking out of a mouth full of teeth. Like a giant blue snail, the head slid across the glass, popped in through the passenger window, and landed laughing in Mellissa's lap. Horrified, she grabbed it and threw it out the window.

Jack screeched the car to a stop in the garage, and for once, the automatic door remote actually worked.

With Herbert and the dog safe in the backyard, Jack and Mellissa proceeded to investigate the house. Everything was silent, no sound, no sign of activity poltergeistian, or otherwise. The hall was silent. In Jack's office, all seemed normal, too. His drawings were still neatly taped to his board; his half-built white model and his expensive client chairs all looked undisturbed.

Jack stopped and whispered, "Do you smell something?"

"I do." Mellissa took a whiff and made a curious face. "What is that?"

They proceeded as quietly as they could, down the hall toward the kitchen, with that sick feeling that says *don't go in there, just run, just get out of the house!* The kitchen was silent, undisturbed, no dishes in the sink or on the dish rack, no pans left on the stove, and the tea towels were neatly folded and hung on the oven handles. And there, on the ahead-of-the-trend avocado Formica island, sat two steaming cups of black coffee, and a plate of fresh warm pastries.

"Beignets." Mellissa took a deep, meditative breath.

"Beignets?"

"Beignets, deep fried, and then rolled in powdered sugar."

Jack started to reach for one. Mellissa stopped him. "Better not."

"You're right."

Neither of them moved.

They looked over the plate and smelled the fried dough, sugar, and cups of morning coffee.

Jack couldn't take it. He grabbed a beignet and took a huge bite before Mellissa could stop him. "Oh my God." His mouth wafted white powder, as he realized how amazing it was.

Mellissa couldn't stand it and took a huge bite, white sugar all over her lips and pajama top. Jack took a huge gulp of coffee. Then Mellissa had a worried look and set down her half-eaten beignet.

She knew one thing about beignets. They had to be served immediately, otherwise they were garbage. Nowhere in the kitchen was there any evidence anyone had been cooking, nor was there a pan, or even a drop of oil, flour, or powdered sugar, anywhere.

Somehow, Sunday, if not exactly normal, at least proceeded. Herbert was surprised at how quickly his parents adapted to seeing the blue ghost dog and started treating him like he was a new member of the family. He focused on dutifully getting his math homework done, with Pierre watching closely and occasionally running away with a page or two in his teeth.

Jack realized that a couple of beignets, coffee, and a shower did wonders for his productivity.

Mellissa stood in front of the refrigerator, her hand on the chevron-shaped stainless-steel handle. She just knew if she opened it, a blue head with flashing eyes was going to jump out at her. She felt like she was constantly turning a crank on a jack-in-the-box, her personal space violated by the threat of a monster jumping from any corner at any moment. She wanted her freedom back, her peace of mind returned to her.

Suddenly the door opened by itself, and she jumped out of her skin, until she realized Herbert was behind her, had opened the door, and was taking out a bottle of milk. He looked at his mother strangely as she nervously reopened the door and peered in, trying to convince herself that there was nothing to fear.

Ghost Dog

Chapter 8

A Secret Shared

Late that night, a few light pebbles tapped Herbert's window. He was too tired to think about it and put his pillow over his head. A few more taps, and some larger pebbles followed. Then a big rock came through, breaking the glass and landing where it woke up Pierre.

Someone outside was getting impatient, Herbert thought. Pierre grabbed the rock, ran to the window, tail wagging, and thinking it was time to play, dropped it.

"Ouch, what the…" said a voice below.

Herbert looked down to the back lawn to where Kasey stood, holding a flashlight and about ready to try a brick.

"I'm sorry your dog is a ghost," Kasey said, as she and Herbert met on the lawn, "but you promised to tell me everything. Did you really think you could keep a ghost dog a secret?"

"I think I could if you would consider keeping your big mouth shut," Herbert said. "I'm sorry, I didn't mean that. There is a bigger problem than the dog now."

"Maybe you're losing your mind a little bit if you think anything could be a bigger problem than having a dog that's a ghost and goes chasing other people's normal dogs around."

"He saved your dog. That's something."

"You're right. I should thank him for that. Where is he?"

"He's right here." Herbert motioned to the ground next to him.

"I don't see anything. Take my hand, Herbert, maybe I can feel him."

Herbert reluctantly took Kasey's hand, and they both came down on their knees. He waved her hand around where Pierre was sitting.

The dog reacted by turning in circles and jumping.

"I felt it!" She tried again. "I feel the air moving. Look, the grass is moving too! This isn't a problem, it's awesome, it's real-life magic."

"He's got friends." Herbert stood. "They're the problem. They've moved in too. Now my parents can see the dog, and they can see these two guys whenever they decide to appear,

which scares the crap out of my mom."

"That's nerve-racking. Weird ghosts hanging around and you don't know where they are," she said. "It's going to take both of us to figure this out. Will you let me in, Herbert, let me in on it, so I can help you?"

Herbert looked at Kasey. In the cold misty air, shivering in her pajamas, she seemed less annoying somehow. Maybe he could trust her, who else if not her?

Suddenly, there was a splash. Pierre ran up to the pool deck, and they followed. They peered over the pool wall, and Herbert saw a blue glow under the water, and they heard a trumpet gurgling.

"He's swimming, the trumpet player is in the pool."

"In the middle of the night?" Kasey looked toward her house, hoping her parents wouldn't wake up. "How do I believe this? How do I know you just haven't lost it?"

The second ghost did a cannonball off the diving board. What Herbert saw was a tall, thin man, giggling like a kid, holding his legs and cutting into the water like a sparkling blue torpedo. All poor Kasey saw was a huge wave of chlorinated water coming out of the darkness. She tried to get away, but she couldn't go fast enough to avoid getting drenched.

In her soaked pajamas, Kasey now looked like a wet cat,

and she was just as pissed. She ran toward her side of the fence.

"You may think this is funny, but you're finished keeping secrets. I'm in this with you, Herbie, and you better get ready, because tomorrow we're solving this, together!" And she was gone.

But the ghost swim party had just started, and since Herbert was already soaked, and Kasey was already mad, he decided to jump in too. It was a raucous late-night swim, and Herbert confirmed that ghosts really do like cold, dark places.

Herbert was worried about his dad. He was always a little worried about him. Sometimes he'd just drift out of a conversation, and Herbert and his mom knew he was forming some kind of creative idea in his head. But now it was worse. The pressures of ghost dogs, headless horn players, supernatural events, psychic therapists, and lack of sleep seemed to be taking their toll. He hoped to keep Pierre out of the way and do his best not to conjure up the other ghosts, at least long enough for his dad to get his work done.

Presently, the most Jack and Mellissa had heard from ghosts was a few echoey cackles out by the pool in the middle of the night, and Mellissa swore she saw ethereal extra socks and long stripped underwear in the clothes dryer.

They both hoped it would all stay that way.

Jack was the most behind on work for his least-favorite clients, Mr. and Mrs. Brawley, and he kept putting them off. When they called, he tried every excuse he could think of, but they insisted on coming over as soon as possible, and that meant tomorrow. Jack had one day to get a week's work done.

Herbert was unusually excited to meet the school bus that day. He wolfed down his breakfast, shared some bacon and toast with Pierre, and went to get his backpack.

Pierre, it had been decided, would stay in Herbert's room until he came home. As a visiting ghost dog, he was not to require any care, and should make a noise only if he absolutely had to go out. Herbert closed the door on the dog's big blue electric eyes, then made a side trip by his dad's studio. He opened his backpack, quietly slipped into Jack's work area, then closed the backpack, and headed back through the kitchen and out the door.

Herbert and Kasey stood a few feet away from each other on the sidewalk, as they always did, and he tried to look like he hardly knew her, as he always did. But when the bus driver closed the door, their typical seat was still unoccupied.

Herbert and Kasey had not gotten on the bus. They had important business to take care of that day.

All stories have a mid-point, and we've reached the mid-point of this one. Herbert had tried to keep his ghost dog a secret from Kasey. But he was about to find out having an ally, especially someone as smart and perceptive as Kasey, could be a tremendous asset. She also asked really good questions that hadn't even occurred to him. But he was going to have to open up and share, something that didn't necessarily come naturally to him.

In the dark recesses of Kasey's garage, behind her father's canvas-covered speedboat on the trailer, behind the old paintings and boxes of holiday decorations, she and Herbert set up their command center. They unloaded and shared the available resources they had gathered, those that were more or less easy to obtain. Kasey had managed to find a couple of research books at the library. She got books on dog behavior, and ghost behavior, but there had been nothing in the card catalog on ghost dogs, or ghosts emanating from amusement park rides. But she did find an authoritative reference that at least based on its age and weight seemed like they should take it seriously: J.W. Wichwar, *The Ghost World: Its Realities, Apparitions & Spooks*, 1919.

"It's old and moldy and disgusting, so I think we should trust it." Kasey had already marked some stories. "Here's one, 'It seems that a dog who is faithful to his master in life, will stay faithful in the afterlife,' well that's sweet."

That was not what Herbert was hoping for. He really wanted to find a way to keep the ghost dog and just get rid of his annoying human ghost intruders.

"It says, 'A ghost may also latch on to someone in the living world, and only appear to them, or sometimes a few people that person loves or is very close to.' That's why you and your parents can see him, and nobody else can!"

"Pierre likes me, and he likes it on our side of the world. The other guys are here for the pool and a free ride. I really hope we can find ways to make them feel less welcome."

Kasey read on. "This is scary. 'There's nothing that keeps a ghost from manipulating things in the real world, they can throw vases, light fires, turn over furniture, and eat food out of your cabinets.' That's so creepy!"

Herbert thought about it. "I've seen Pierre eat, drink water, pee, he can track mud in, and those guys can make waves in the pool too."

"Okay, I almost believe you." Kasey rolled her eyes.

Herbert pulled out a wrinkled guide map of Disneyland, and they looked closely at the area around the Haunted Mansion and New Orleans Square. "It just looks like it's a little white house, but when you're inside, it goes on and on. I don't know how they have all the ghosts, all the rooms. It's got to be huge." He pulled out a sheet of white cardboard. On it, Herbert had sketched a kind of treasure map recalling everything he remembered about where they had gone on the ride.

"My dad's an architect. He says everything makes more sense in a model," he said as he pulled out more cardboard, a matte knife, and a bottle of white glue, all secretly *borrowed* from his father's office.

Kasey and Herbert went to work. Kasey found some old plywood boards and duct tape to seal up their command center. She made notes from the books and hung them across the wall, capturing bits of historical information, as well as tips for psychics trying to get rid of ghosts.

Having a fastidious architect at home had given Herbert an appreciation of historical architecture, art, and even how many stairs it takes to go to another floor. He had a neatness and process about him that meant a sharp pencil with ruled lines, clean cuts of cardboard, and tiny amounts of glue, even if he had to wait a long time for things to dry.

Kasey was a rocket-fast reader and could extract key points from research and summarize them quickly on note cards. She also brought out a ball of red twine, and used it to link thoughts together, making the boards a map of information the same way the model was a map of the physical world Herbert had experienced.

Bit by bit their room was taking shape. Kasey rolled in an old wheelbarrow, and it made a perfect table to elevate Herbert's model. Between Kasey's creatively linked and taped research boards, and Herbert's perfect white model, a story was beginning to form, even if it was a long way from being understood.

Next door, Jack's day was not going as well at all. "They've stolen everything!"

"Now take it one by one, Jack. What are you missing?"

"I told you those ghosts are trying to sabotage my meeting. Everything I need is missing!" *Everything,* it turned out, was anything on the critical path of finishing his work by tomorrow's client meeting.

"There, see, my glue is gone." It was. "My cardboard has disappeared." Most of the stack was depleted. "Knife, pencils, they know." He looked around the room, trying to connect with the otherworldly spirits. "They know what I need," he spoke loudly as if he wanted the ghosts to hear him through the walls. "And they're going to make sure I don't get it done."

Jack promised to stay calm, and focus on his drawings, while Mellissa drove to the store. On her list were white glue, illustration board, a new matte knife, and everything she would need to make a nice, clean, stacked tray of finger sandwiches for the client meeting. She had in mind bread, with the crust cut off, cucumbers, cream cheese, ham, smoked salmon, and those tiny, spicy pickles she loved saying to herself in an exaggerated French accent, *cornichons piquants*. She planned to spice things up by mixing iced tea and lemonade, and Jack, they planned, would offer to spike it for the Brawleys with a little something from the bar cabinet.

The store was brightly lit, and there were people all around, talking and laughing, nothing to be afraid of. Mellissa thought she heard a few echoey cackles among the English muffins, but the grocery store otherwise seemed normal, so she was sure it was her imagination. She got some bread and headed for the office supply section, where she picked out Elmer's glue, some white cardboard, and a new matte knife. She pushed on, heading toward the condiments aisle. As she whirled along, crossing items off her list, she didn't notice what a toddler in the cart behind her did. Her glue bottle levitated out of the cart and neatly landed itself back on the shelf. The kid went crazy with laughter. Mellissa smiled and made eye contact with the toddler long enough to miss seeing the whiteboard and the matte knife quickly floating back to their shelves as well. But the toddler saw it and found it hysterical. The mom gave Mellissa a curious look, and they rolled on past her.

At the butcher counter, a man was ordering andouille sausage. He gave Mellissa a polite smile, as she ordered a half pound of thin-sliced smoked salmon. She looked down nervously at her cart, and then inside her bag as if some big blue ghost might jump out at her. The butcher set down the salmon and the sausage packages. In a split second, an invisible force reached in and switched them. The man thought his package felt a little light. Mellissa was so busy watching out for ghost shoppers, she didn't notice hers was pretty heavy.

The search for the *cornichons piquants* took a while. As she moved her cart along searching the shelves, a number of items levitated off the shelves and made their way into Mellissa's cart. From the aisle behind her, additions floated in: saffron, paprika, cayenne pepper, cumin, and a small bag of expensive Spanish rice hitting the bottom of the cart so hard that Mellissa jumped. She looked around at the spicy additions, then looked around the store. She pulled on the rice, but it refused to move. She pulled it again, impossible. "Come on, I don't need this," she said aloud. The lady with the toddler came by, and Mellissa decided to put off the rice struggle.

She moved forward and finally saw the *cornichons piquants.* She reached up but something was odd. There was a glow coming from behind it. The sharp beam of light cut through the spaces between the green vinegar and tiny floating cucumbers. She tried to pull away but found herself drawn to it, her hand moved toward the little jar, pulled by an unseen force. She finally pulled it away, and behind it, there was a bright light, and two big eyes, staring back at her. She screamed and pulled back, dropping the jar and spilling pickles all over the floor.

"I'm sorry." From behind the shelf, a grocery clerk

turned off his flashlight and stopped taking inventory on the other side. He rushed around, helped Mellissa steer clear of the briny glass mess, got her a new jar, then led her safely to the checkout area. "Is there anything else I can do for you?" he asked.

Mellissa looked nervously around. "No. Well, actually is anything strange going on today?"

"In this place?" He laughed. "Every day!"

Mellissa felt in a daze and just stared up at the ceiling. She absentmindedly gave the checker some cash, took her change, took a deep breath, and bravely carted her way out of there.

Jack looked out the window when he heard the school bus pull away. As usual, he saw Herbert with his backpack coming down the driveway, and Kasey coming down hers, both acting very much like they didn't know each other. By the time Herbert was at the front door, Jack could already hear Pierre yipping. "Take the dog out and I'll make us a peanut butter and mayonnaise sandwich. How about it?"

Herbert sneaked past his room and made a quick stop in his father's studio, returning the glue bottle, remaining white boards and scraps, and knife. Then he raced back to his room and ran Pierre to the backyard.

Mellissa pulled into the garage, looked around, grabbed her bags quickly and rushed out the side door before the garage door closed. She took a breath of relief that nothing weird was happening in there. Herbert was running in the backyard with a ghost dog, but that seemed pretty normal now.

She set her bags down on the counter and shuffled through one, then another. She checked her list. "I forgot the boards, the glue, and the knife. I've got to drive back."

Jack looked up, stressed. "That's why you went in the first place. How did you possibly forget?"

"I also went to get the sandwiches and tea for your clients. Remember?"

"My clients? You mean, *our* clients?"

She said, "I'm going back."

"Great, another hour lost on the model, thank you." Jack stomped back to his office, leaving his sandwiches half completed.

Mellissa was not happy. She grabbed her keys, ready to leave, just as Jack came back into the kitchen.

"Wait!" Jack said, holding the matte knife, cardboard, and his glue bottle.

"You put us all through this. Couldn't you look more carefully before you start a fire drill?"

"I guess I just didn't see them."

"You thought it was easier to blame ghosts, or me, or anybody. It couldn't possibly be your distracted mind? Maybe you're locked up in that room too much to see what's really going on around here."

"I'm beginning to believe those ghosts were never here. We just imagined them, it's a stress reaction, to everything, including to the dog." Then Jack realized the sandwiches he had started were not just finished, but also sliced in half and put on nice plates with doilies. He took a bite. *Perfect*, he thought.

Mellissa spread her groceries on the kitchen counter and perfectly aligned them, organized by type and size. She didn't recognize anything. "Don't be so sure they're not real."

"Why?"

She showed him what was on the counter, the spices, the andouille sausage. "I don't think the Brawleys will be having finger sandwiches."

The next day Herbert woke up early, took Pierre out, made his own cereal, and slipped out without any inquiries. "I've got a big science project," he told his mom.

Jack watched from his window as Herbert ran down toward the bus. He wished he had hugged him, or that it could be Saturday, so they could've just gone out and had some fun together. He looked back down at his drawing, not seeing Herbert and Kasey ditch the bus, and run back down her driveway.

They sneaked along the hedge between the two properties and back through the side door of her garage. The command center had really expanded. Kasey found some discarded lamps to light their boards, and they'd rigged up a string of big bulb holiday lights that gave the room an appropriate blue glow. But their real effort was on the model. It had taken them both, cutting cardboard, holding pieces while the glue dried, tearing parts up, modifying, and gluing again. Now it stood there, elevated on the wheelbarrow, the Haunted Mansion, exactly assembled from Herbert's memory of his two traumatic visits. There was the Mansion itself, visible in the guide map, but Herbert had remembered a stretching room, a long hallway, and then the ride running through a vast night scene. He had added all this on the other side of the railroad tracks because it seemed like the only way it could fit in that area of Disneyland. The "Museum of the Weird" construction area, where they held the séance, he located below ground in a crypt area beneath the entrance, and crossing over to connect to the graveyard, there was a giant ballroom, where the dancers were.

"It's complicated." Herbert studied the model.

"That's an understatement."

"I mean, hard to build, so many levels, up and down. If my dad were here, he'd be worried about how to keep the rain out."

Kasey shouted, "That's it!"

"What?"

"If you can keep the rain out, you can keep everything else in!" she said.

"Like what?" Herbert was confused.

"We're going to the building department," she ordered. "Go put on some nice clothes."

"Why?"

"Your dad's an architect, drawings, we need to find the drawings."

"To see how they keep the rain out?"

"We need to find out how they keep the ghosts *in*. That might tell us how your ghosts got *out*!"

Jack left early to get drawings printed, and with Herbert gone too, Mellissa realized it was the first time she'd been alone in the house since the *appearances*. She suddenly felt a shiver, a sense she was not alone. She whistled nervously as she walked down, opened Herbert's door, and let the dog run after her. Recognizing the uniqueness of the opportunity, Pierre decided to be on his best behavior. He sat nicely next to the kitchen table, tail wagging, front paws folded, modest, attentive, a friend, but not in the way.

"Good dog." Mellissa was thankful for a little company. *Even the ghost of a dog could be a friend*, she thought. She opened the refrigerator slowly, and seeing no one, pulled out bread, a half-consumed cucumber, and some cold cuts. She took two fancy glass pitchers out of the cabinet, sliced some lemons to put in one, and filled the other with tea bags. Then she started the stove and put on a teakettle.

As she turned back to the counter, she realized the wrapped bundle of sausage was sitting there and she hadn't remembered taking it out. She looked down at Pierre. "Did you take this out?" Pierre just licked his lips.

She put it back into the refrigerator and grabbed the cream cheese and mayonnaise while she was at it. When she turned back to the counter, saffron, paprika, cayenne pepper, cumin, and the bag of Spanish rice were all lined up perfectly in her work area.

She looked at Pierre again, and he just went down on his front paws and growled. She tried to back away but couldn't. Her feet were frozen. She tried to pick up the ingredients one by one, but they stuck to the counter like magnets. The bread package split open, and slices started to jump, like popping toast, landing one by one in the garbage bin, the lid opening just in time to devour each one. The teakettle started to boil, and from deep within it, a whistling sound started. It started low, then built into an earsplitting crescendo. Pierre began to bark.

The refrigerator started to shake, and it shook more and more violently until the door popped open. Right in front of her eyes, a sharp cleaver levitated, floated toward her, and the handle landed in her hand. Her fingers involuntarily snapped tight around it. She was about to bring the cleaver down on the cutting board when Pierre jumped into the refrigerator and grabbed the sausage package in his teeth. He jumped up on the cutting board, tore the paper off the package, and jumped out of the way, clearing his tail with a little yip, just as Mellissa's hand involuntarily brought the cleaver down hard on the sausage and chopped it.

She chopped and chopped, the ghost dog barked, and the teakettle whistle continued to screech.

Chapter 9

The Search for Answers

Kasey made Herbert sneak out of the house wearing his once-a-year suit, and she managed to put something together for herself that communicated the casual creative style of a woman professional in the design world.

Neither outfit worked at the desk of the Anaheim Building Department. "How can I help you children?"

Children! Their plans crushed, Kasey pivoted quickly.

"We need to see the plans for the recently constructed

Haunted Mansion at Disneyland."

When the clerk didn't react, she continued.

"It's an authorized research project."

"The plans are not available to just anyone who walks in, they're official, and usually have information not available to the public."

"Oh, we know that! Got to be secure, can't be too careful these days." She elbowed Herbert, who agreed, and took his cue.

"Of course, and we have the authorization through WED Enterprises. They authorized us, I mean they've given us their authorization," Herbert struggled.

"They're cool with it," Kasey said confidently. She elbowed Herbert again, and he remembered to pull the card out.

"He even gave us his card." Herbert handed the plain white card over:

Kasey whispered, "WED stands for Walter Elias Disney. It's his top-secret design company."

The clerk studied the card for a moment, and then gave a skeptical smile. "Mr. Grimsley, such a nice gentleman."

"Yeah, 'Grim' we call him," Kasey offered.

"Yes, he's a little dark on the humor side! We've seen him quite often recently." Her tone became a little more responsive. "Now, what is it you want?"

"We need all the drawings for the Haunted Mansion structure," Kasey started.

"The plan," Herbert specified from listening to his dad. "And the roof plan, something to show how they keep the weather out."

"Something to show how they keep all that magic in." Kasey lowered her voice and raised the stakes.

"None of us has actually seen the ride yet," the clerk said. "Have you?"

"Well, of course, I have, and everyone that's working on it has," Herbert said proudly.

"I'll tell Mr. Grimsley he absolutely must include you in the preview invitations." Kasey decided to go for broke.

It turned out the possibility of an invitation to the hottest new ticket in town worked, and they soon found themselves seated around a big table with thick rolls of blueprints around them.

As Herbert paged through the drawings, Kasey started to read through a thick binder titled *Project Description*.

"The main house is to represent a typical New Orleans–style, three-story, square, brick structure built around the late 1700s or early 1800s. It has a two-story addition at the rear and a flat hipped roof surrounded by a cupola with a gilded weather vane and three round-arch windows. The tympanum—I have no idea what that is—of the two-story columned portico is decorated with rays radiating from a half sun. Elaborate cast-iron grillwork will characterize three sides of the house, especially around the two-story gallery porches. The Beauregard House, on Chartres Street, is a typical model for this kind of structure."

Herbert found a plan of the main level. "This is where we entered. I remember that well enough."

Kasey continued, "To gain the space necessary for all of the show elements, the main house will mask an extensive network of underground and hidden show facilities, unseen by the public but entered and exited by means of the main mansion. An extensive graveyard and large moss-covered trees will simulate an austere New Orleans setting."

"That's exactly what I thought. We have to find all those networks of show plans, hidden tunnels. Where are they?" Herbert looked through the drawings, but everything seemed to relate to a normal house. He flipped along the sheet titles at the outside edge. "Found it! Show plan! Graveyard plan!"

"Shhhhh!" Kasey reminded Herbert there were people at other tables and they were starting to take interest in what these exceedingly young architects were up to.

Herbert slid his hand under the titles that indicated "Show," and slowly rolled the pages back to reveal them. They both stood there, ready to see a great secret revealed.

"Nothing," Herbert said.

"What's all that area?"

"Nothing. The drawing shows nothing." Herbert traced the drawing with his finger, there was the edge of a big building, much larger than the mansion, some columns, some big doors, and some curved dotted lines indicating a ride path. Other than that, the page was empty.

"What's this?" Kasey found a note in the center of a large white space, neatly lettered, with arrows pointing all around it. "It says, 'For show building details, see WED Drawings,' this is just the building, they kept all the secrets. This was a pointless trip."

"Hold on a second." Kasey looked closer at the title block. "Show me that card again!" The project designer was listed on the drawings as Marc Grimsley.

"That's the guy," Herbert matched the name on the card. The title also listed WED ENTERPRISES and an address he quickly copied down on the back of the card.

The Search for Answers

The pot on the stove was bubbling, and a simply heavenly, earthy smell was coming from it. Across the counter were plates and cutting boards, filled with scraps from pulverized ingredients. Mellissa put the scraps of andouille sausage on the floor for Pierre to devour. She surveyed her other preparations. They had gotten bolder as she went along. What began as an insane attack on sausage, had been followed by the chopping of hot peppers and onions, the slaughtering of tomatoes, and spices thrown in without any attempt to measure them. In the final throes of her possessed cooking, she had robbed the freezer of frozen shrimp, and even some chicken stolen out of a frozen dinner. Everything had been mixed together in the intense caldron that now wafted an amazing smell.

Mellissa had tasted the brew, and the hot peppers and spices had burned her mouth but within seconds her brain exchanged the intense feeling of fire for a sense of total euphoria. She wanted to keep on cooking or do something really wild like run around the yard with Pierre in her bare feet.

"*Ça c'est bon!*"

Mellissa heard someone speak, and it wasn't Jack.

"*Ça c'est bon!*"

She slowly turned. The two ghosts were right there,

standing over her stove as her mother and sister did on holidays. They had wooden spoons and were tasting the pot. They spoke, obviously critiquing her cooking, but she had no idea what they were saying.

Her instinct was to run, but she felt emboldened.

"*Ça c'est bon!*" The soldier spoke first, a huge smile.

"*Ça c'est bon!*" The short man joined in.

"*Ça va?*" Mellissa didn't quite believe she was conversing in French with a couple of ghosts.

"*Ah oui, ça c'est bon,*" he answered.

"*Ça...c'est...bon,*" she tried.

"*Ah oui, ça c'est bon!*"

"We seem to be getting somewhere." Mellissa was warming up.

"*Bon appétit!*" they responded.

"Oh, I know that." She took another taste of the sauce. "*Bon appétit!*"

The trumpeter started playing a Cajun traditional song, and Pierre began barking.

"*Laissez les bons temps rouler!*"

Mellissa had no idea that what she was hearing was the Cajun equivalent of "let the good times roll!" She was sharing a spoon of incredibly spicy jambalaya with two ghosts in her kitchen, and she didn't even know how it got there. Somehow, she had channeled the culinary knowledge from one or both of these glowing gentlemen, and now her kitchen was a complete wreck, her husband was away, and he and his clients were expected at any moment. And yet, there she was, and she really *did* want to *let the good times roll.* In fact, she wanted the good times to roll like she'd never even imagined before. If she had known where to go, she would have gone out right then and gotten a tattoo.

It was a long bus ride from Anaheim to Glendale, but Kasey had insisted they had no choice. She said they were on the verge of a major discovery, and explorers on the verge of a discovery didn't just go home and wait for another day.

The bus stopped right across the street from the address Herbert had copied from the drawings. They stood on the corner for a few minutes, watching the comings and goings of people.

"It looks so boring," Herbert said, as he carefully watched the nondescript building. No one looked like an inventor or a ghost scientist or a spiritualist. For the most part, they looked like plain old regular people, in fact more casual than either Kasey or Herbert expected.

"Let's go in." Kasey had her nerve up. "Just act natural, like we work here."

"No one is going to believe we work here!" Herbert tried to put some reality into Kasey's boldness. "It already didn't work in Anaheim."

"We got the drawings, didn't we? Come on!"

It turned out that Herbert's sense of professionalism was keener than Kasey's, honed by occasional visits to clients with his father. Herbert knew something about the business world, and no matter how casual, they didn't expect school kids to just come traipsing in, unless they were on an organized field trip.

"Do you have an appointment?" At the front desk was an efficient-looking woman with a name tag that said *Millie*. Someone with the name Millie might not have seemed to Kasey or Herbert to be an all-powerful guard against the outside world. But no one, it seemed, underestimated Millie, or expected to pass her station without authorization. Kasey now worried the lobby might be as far as they could go after their long bus ride. But she was determined. She decided the idea that they were adults was not worth pursuing.

"We're doing a school report."

"How nice. What grade?"

"Ninth." Herbert figured he put on a suit, so why waste the chance to exaggerate a little.

The dreaded standard operating line came back nonetheless. "And do you have an appointment?"

"Actually, it's too soon to have an appointment." Kasey leaned in, secretively. "This is about the Haunted Mansion."

"Well, I'd like to help you. What is the topic: story, show, special effects, design?"

"How about ghost security?" Herbert was done messing around.

"I'm quite sure we have no one who's responsible for that. Perhaps you want to call Disneyland. Thank you so much for coming by." She smiled with a smile that said, *Kids, this is the end of the road.*

Desperate, Herbert remembered the card and showed it to Millie.

"He told me if I had any questions, or suggestions, to just give him a call."

"Well, Mr. Grimsley is a nice gentleman, but he never takes visitors, especially not unexpected ones. I'm so sorry for the misunderstanding." And there came that smile again.

Scram!

Kasey and Herbert felt they had exhausted any potential to get around Millie. The calling card, the ace in the hole, had not worked. They started to turn toward the door, but Herbert had one more try.

"Could you tell Mr. Grimsley that I have his dog?"

Millie for the first time looked at least a little befuddled. "You have his what?"

"*We* have his dog," Kasey confirmed.

Millie dialed a number and spoke very quietly to the party on the other end of the line. She hung up the phone and handed them a sign-in sheet. "Fill in your full names, and a current address." Then she handed them two visitor passes. "Mr. Grimsley will see you now."

Ghost Dog

Chapter 10

The Inner Workings of WED

Herbert and Kasey thought they won a grand prize. Not only had they been given two visitor passes, but an intern was assigned to lead them right to the person who was likely to understand all of their problems. Herbert thought it was really cool to have someone assigned to give them a tour on the way. Kasey suspected the intern was just a spy, making sure they didn't cause any trouble.

As soon as they passed Millie's station, the nondescript

building came to life like nothing either of them had ever seen before. If Santa had a workshop, if Charlie really had a Chocolate Factory, if Oz had really been a wondrous land, they might have come close to the inner workings of Walter Elias Disney Enterprises, also known as WED.

The intern led them down a long hallway with small offices on each side, and large panels, each panel filled with dozens of small drawings, like little cartoons. The WED people were talking excitedly, pointing, and telling stories as they moved sketch by sketch along the boards. A few of them had rulers and slide rules, they argued about details, and they wrote little notes in the margins of the sketches. They seemed to love to argue, and the more dramatic the better. Periodically an announcer would come on, "Wathel Rogers, please call the operator." This was, without a doubt, a busy place.

Out the back doors of the main building was a vast, treeless black asphalt service yard. Around it were projects on trucks and forklifts, with workers rolling them around, painting details, fixing mechanical parts, and doing what they seemed to do the best, arguing about every detail.

There was a huge portable backyard pool. This was no technical astronaut training pool, but a big plastic-lined pool that looked like it came right out of Sears. In the pool were two elephants, robots that is, and the mother elephant was washing off her rubbery baby with water from her trunk. In the pool with them was a large man holding a hose with valves and dressed in waders like he was on a trout-fishing expedition. Everywhere Kasey and Herbert looked there were skyway buckets, train cars, and they had to jump out of the way as a big truck pulled out, a large dinosaur strapped in the flatbed.

The largest building had a big sign that read MAPO, and a picture of Mary Poppins, flying with her umbrella above it. The intern filled them in. "MAPO is where we build the really secret stuff. It was built when Walt had enough money saved up after Mary Poppins was successful."

Based on the inside of this building it looked like Mary Poppins must have sold a lot of tickets and popcorn. The two-story space was filled with machines making whizzing air sounds, and there was a giant yellow crane with flashing lights delivering part of a monorail train to the center aisle. The intern led them up a ramp into the office area. Along the ramp were human figures, but made of clear plastic, with complex mechanical parts inside. But their faces were realistic.

"That's one of the Pirates." Herbert was excited like it was a friend he recognized. "What's he doing here?"

"Almost everything here is headed to Florida," the intern whispered an aside, "but that's really confidential."

"You can trust us," Kasey assured.

At the top of the ramp was a bird inside a glass case. Kasey, the intern, and Herbert grouped around it. It looked natural, just like a stuffed bird in a museum. A gentleman walking by stopped, flipped a switch, and the bird started moving realistically. "A bird has five motions," he said. "That's all it takes to make you think it's real."

Herbert and Kasey had no way of knowing it, but this was not just a nice man who saw a couple of visitors while he was on his way to a meeting. This man in the short-sleeved blue striped shirt, with a few pens in his pocket protector, was likely a mechanical genius yet never thought twice about being one. "It turns out it is pretty easy to make things look hard," he said, "but it is very hard to make things look easy." And he was on his way. This bird looked easy, but it was because this man and his other collaborators only loved mechanical parts when they could be cobbled together to tell a story.

"Making a random pile of pipes, aluminum and steel parts, and a few fake feathers look like a bird tells a story," explained the intern. "Tells it in such a way that your critical mind shuts down, and your imagination says that is the most magical bird I have ever seen. That bird could be my friend." Without expecting to, Kasey and Herbert had just seen true magic at work.

"Shall we move on?" The intern was efficient, but she also knew visitors sometimes needed a moment to absorb, to soak it in; everyone, whether they bought a ticket or not, deserved a little magic once in a while. For one moment, Herbert wondered, *Could it be that the ghost dog is just magic, or some kind of trick that I hadn't been able to figure out yet?*

At the very top of the ramp was a cubicle with yet another reception person. Kasey whispered, "We're here to see Mr. Grimsley."

"Down the corridor, first door on your left."

From the top floor they could look down at everything they'd just seen. In front of them was a darkened office, with the name plate, Marc Grimsley, and beneath it a skeleton's hand held a sign that read GO AWAY. The intern even looked nervous, but she knocked. "Mr. Grimsley?"

"Come in." He sounded friendly enough, but his office was quite dark. "Come in," his voice echoed and sounded a little impatient. The intern went first, inching around the corner, leading Kasey, and Herbert, who hung back, trying to get his eyes adjusted to the dark.

"Welcome, foolish mortals," a voice said. They rounded the corner and found a bust of a dour-looking man, carved in stone.

"Step all the way in, please." The stone-carved face not only talked but also followed them in, its eyes tracking their motion perfectly. "Welcome to my office. How can I help you, or how can I help you *out*?" The voice laughed ironically. Kasey was scared now and stood behind Herbert, who stepped forward, determined not to be intimidated by this jokester.

"Mr. Grimsley, I have your dog!"

There was a pause, the stone face stopped moving, frozen in mid-expression, and the office light came on.

"Hello, I am Marc Grimsley, and I am afraid I don't have a dog."

Marc had a deep voice, and spoke with seriousness, although there was just a little sly ironic smile in there too. On his walls were sketches, copied articles, and photos of ghosts, graveyards, and scary-looking houses. He even had a copy of the J.W. Wichwar book, *The Ghost World: Its Realities, Apparitions & Spooks*, that Kasey recognized immediately.

"He has your dog, I've seen it. Or at least my dog has, but I've seen him slobber and move things."

"Tell me, this dog, mister...?"

"Herbert."

"And I'm Kasey, Herbert's best friend."

"Nice to meet you Herbert, and Kasey his best friend. Now tell me about this dog."

"He's blue, his eyes have lightning flashes, and you can see through him." Herbert wanted to get it all in. "I named him Pierre, but I don't really know if that's his name, but he answers to it anyway."

"And how did you ever come across such a dog, Herbert?"

"We went to the Haunted Mansion, my ride just floated above the track, and the dog saw me, so he followed me."

Grimsley looked curiously at Herbert like he had met him somewhere before.

"We tried to take him back and he followed us home a second time."

"Hold on. Our ride never levitates or otherwise wanders off the track, it's impossible from an engineering point of view, and he followed you, how?"

"I don't know how, in our car on the way home, I guess, but he showed up at our house that night. And then we..."

Kasey tried to pick up. "Tried to return him, but he..."

"Followed us home again. But that's not the worst of

it."

Grimsley looked like he couldn't possibly imagine what else there could be if that was not the worst of it.

"He brought two friends back with him. The first time I was the only one who could see Pierre, now my parents can see him, and they can see the other guys too."

"Tell me about the other guys."

Herbert started to explain, but Grimsley was hardly listening. He looked like his mind was jumbling up with all the implausible details. He reached out for a leather-bound sketch book, and a soft pencil.

"Okay, now let's just say I believed you, which I do not, describe to me in detail, everything, please. And like all good stories, let's start from the beginning."

Herbert started from the beginning. He described the dog, its shape, size, eyes, tail, the way he moved, and the lightning sparks he made with his eyes. Grimsley, being a fast sketch artist, drew all the details dutifully with a thick, soft pencil. The dog took shape on the page, along with the two cypress trees. He made action marks next to the tail and added a lightning effect across the eyes.

"Like this?"

"That's him!"

"Okay now, what about the others?"

Grimsley listened carefully. He sketched out the details as Herbert described them. First, he blocked in the ghost troubadours with bright red eyes, and blue transparent skins. He colored in the eyes and blue glow with markers. He added more detail as Herbert described the short man with a stocking cap and the big trumpet, and the thin man in uniform complete with a bicorn hat and gold epaulets, plucking away at his lyre. Herbert described him as a little bonkers, so Grimsley put hypnotic spirals in his eyes.

Grimsley held up the sketch. "Does this look right, about how you saw it?"

"Exactly! That's them, even Pierre's lightning blue eye flashes!"

Grimsley set the sketchbook down on the table and put his pencil and markers back in the cup. He looked seriously at Herbert, a grave look that only Grimsley had the

years, and the gloomy personality, to draw forth.

"I have some bad news for you, Herbert. I know every square inch of that ride, and these characters, as you describe them, are not there, and they never have been. I've never seen them before. And even if they were, they'd be bolted to the floor. They don't just go wandering off."

"But that's not possible." Kasey jumped to Herbert's defense.

"Have you actually seen them?"

Kasey had to admit, "No, but I've been splashed by them, and Pierre helped my dog when she was trapped."

"But have you seen them?" Kasey couldn't say she had.

Grimsley shifted his eyes over to Herbert and pulled up whatever warmth he could muster, along with, what for him was, a knowing half-smile. "Look, kid, I love this stuff, just look around my office. I love scary. I love to be scared and I love to scare people. It's in our nature. For thousands of years, we've told ghost stories around the fire, and no matter how much we want them to be, they're not real, they're just made up. And here, we're great at it, we make magic so people will believe it, but it's not real, not one bit of it."

"But you don't understand, Mr. Grimsley. Our house

has been a living hell, I'm not joking. The dog was one thing, but these other guys are freeloaders, my mom is freaked out, my dad can't get his work done, and if I don't help him, he could lose his business. That's not made up, not any of that, either." Herbert stood his ground, waiting for Grimsley to respond.

But if there was one thing Grimsley had learned in his many years of working in the business world, it was how to slip out of a meeting when he needed to. He excused himself and stepped out of the office for a moment. He handed five dollars to the intern. "Take them by the gift shop. No one should ever come by without visiting the gift shop." And then Mr. Grimsley was on his way down the maze of offices and cubicles and gone.

"Mr. Grimsley had to go to another meeting, but let's continue our tour."

Grimsley stood back on a second-floor balcony where he could see the intern lead Kasey and Herbert out the big service doors back toward the main office. His normally grim look turned ever grimmer and seemed to suggest more concern than he had let on. He worked his way back to his office, and inside, took out a key and opened a flat cabinet filled with sketches of various sizes and levels of completion.

He reached under some of them and pulled out a drawing. He placed it next to the sketch he had just done while talking to Herbert. The characters and the setting were exactly the same.

Grimsley came out of his office and locked the door. He turned around a door handle sign that said DO NOT DISTURB.

On the other side it said GONE TO DISNEYLAND.

On his way out, Grimsley stopped by Millie's desk and had a few laughs with her. When she turned around to get a phone call, he took the top sheet off her visitor sign-in clipboard, slipped it into his pocket, and rushed out.

Chapter 11

Sous-Chefs

Mellissa stood in the kitchen. She no longer had any fear of ghosts, or anything jumping out at her. The dishes were done and put away. There was no spilled sauce on the counters. In fact, the kitchen was spotless. She had no idea how the kitchen had gotten this way, and at the moment she didn't really care. A visit from the afterlife, by two young gentleman sous-chefs speaking French, helping her cook and clean up, didn't seem scary at all anymore. She decided that the two chefs' names were likely Jérôme and Fabien, or at least those were as good as any. Should they appear again, to guide her through the creation of a beef bourguignon, she planned on having a lot more fun; given another opportunity, she would be *sans frein*, or in her thinking, a lot less *restrained*.

"What's that smell?" Jack had appeared in the doorway. For a moment he didn't look like Mellissa's stressed-out husband, but more like the handsome Jack she had met fifteen years ago.

"It's jambalaya." The sound rolled across her tongue, leaving her mouth in the perfect position to plant a romantic kiss on Jack's.

The doorbell rang.

"The Brawleys."

"Whatever is that smell, dear?" Mrs. Brawley noticed as she stepped in the door.

"Jambalaya," Mellissa said. She did not pronounce it with the same sultriness she had used with Jack.

"Well, whatever it is, I hope it doesn't go into the finger sandwiches!" Mr. Brawley was gruff from the beginning, and because he was rude to Mellissa, her two new friends Jérôme and Fabien, watched his every move.

The meeting was off to a difficult start.

The Brawleys settled into the leather client chairs directly in front of Jack's model and drawings, and the ghosts stood a watchful eye right behind them.

"You guys were not invited," Mellissa blurted out toward the ghosts.

"You invited us. If you wanted us to come at another time…" said Mr. Brawley, indignant.

"You are here at the exact right time," Jack took over. "You said you wanted a house that was adventurous. Well, I think I've got something you're really going to like." Jack began his pitch.

"Actually, I said distinctive, not adventurous," Mr. Brawley started in. "*Distinctive* means you worked with an architect, and it doesn't look like everyone else's house, *adventurous* means you probably spent too much money and it took too long."

Jack moved the model toward the Brawleys.

Jérôme appeared above Mr. Brawley's head, where Jack could not see him, but Mellissa could. The ghost made a mean face and picked up the glue bottle, contemplating pouring a few big gobs on Mr. Brawley's comb-over.

"Don't you dare touch that," Mellissa said sharply, trying to stop Jérôme's mischief. Jack looked at her shocked.

"Well, I wasn't going to touch it," Mr. Brawley said, shocked at her tone. "I thought Jack wanted us to look."

"I do," said Jack, correcting Mellissa. "Have a close look." Jack moved the model closer to Mr. Brawley, trying to fend off a bad situation. Fabien from right behind Jack shoved Jack's elbow, which made him force the model right into the client's lap, a few pieces of wood and cardboard cracking in the process.

"I told you to stay away and not touch anything!" Mellissa tried to talk quietly through her teeth, but it was audible by everyone.

"He shoved it right at me," Mr. Brawley pushed the model back, struggled to squeeze himself out of the leather chair, stood, and dusted debris from his slacks.

"My fault." Jack proceeded over to the drawing, trying to get Mellissa, whatever was up with her, out of the main view. "The nature of this adventurous design is the complex rooms and balconies."

"*Adventurous*. See, Jack, you don't listen. I said distinctive." He sat back down in a huff, a huff powerful enough to do the rest of the work tearing the leather strap that the ghost dog had started by chewing it a few days before. As the strap tore, poor Mr. Brawley's oversized butt dropped about a foot down into the structure of the broken chair. Jack went quickly to help extract him.

"This whole meeting is an adventure," Mr. Brawley growled as he stood. Mrs. Brawley subtly checked the back of his pants to make sure they hadn't split. Laughter being the contagion that it is, Mellissa had an impossible time keeping herself together because the ghosts had gone into hysterics.

"I think it's time for a little refreshment, don't you?" Mellissa needed an escape. The two ghosts thought it was an excellent idea and floated over to the bar, sticking their blue fingers into the icy pitchers, and licking them. Fabien cracked some ice in his teeth, which had the Brawleys seen it, looked like ice was cracking in midair, and falling into the glasses. Mellissa tried to block the view of the ghosts goofing around the bar. "This is not for you!"

By now the Brawleys were confused and getting plenty anxious.

"Oh, she means me. If she's not careful I'll eat and drink everything before you even get here." Jack softened his language and tried presenting the key elements in more practical terms, hoping to nurture a casual, conversational environment. "Anyone want their tea or lemonade spiked a little?" Mr. Brawley would have, but the look from Mrs.

Brawley didn't approve.

"We've got another engagement immediately after this," Mr. Brawley offered sternly.

As Jack got down to business, Mellissa finished putting ice in glasses and didn't notice Jérôme as he emptied the full contents of a bar bottle directly into both the lemonade and the tea pitchers.

"Very refreshing," said Mrs. Brawley.

Mr. Brawley tried restarting with a more casual tone. He made a toast, and then took a huge gulp. "A little sweet, but all right." Mrs. Brawley was pleasant as always, even a little giddy, but Mr. Brawley started to get a bit negative, and nitpicked at little details.

His first concern was washing the windows. "No way to get to them. They'll always be unsightly," he critiqued. The driveway was too short, the garage too narrow, and the curvy construction way too expensive.

Jack knew enough about landscaping to know when things were going downhill. He looked at Mellissa desperately.

"How about some jambalaya? It's all made." She was sure this was the big save.

Mrs. Brawley was a little nervous about it. "As long as

it's not too spicy. His stomach is so sensitive."

As Mellissa got bowls, and put a bit of rice in each one, she threatened the ghosts from the safety of the kitchen. "One more thing and you're both getting locked in the dryer!" They didn't seem to be around, so she didn't really even know if they heard her.

What she didn't notice as she was lecturing was an extra ingredient coming out of the cabinet, Tabasco sauce. In the hands of offended, protective spirits, who had already demonstrated a penchant for spreading terror, Tabasco sauce could become a licensable weapon, and unknown to Mellissa, Mr. Brawley's bowl, had become the target.

By the time Mellissa returned, they appeared to be making some progress, a break seemed welcome, and Mrs. Brawley even complimented the jambalaya as unexpectedly tasty. Things just seemed to be going better. But Mr. Brawley became quiet, a bit too quiet.

Three things were at work in poor Mr. Brawley's stomach. First, he was not aware his pleasant tea and lemonade mixture had been spiked. Second, a practical-joking spirit had added a dose of red pepper sauce into his aromatic jambalaya. And third, the day before, he had contracted one of Jack's competing architects to carry forward his and his wife's dream house, and he had really come over to tell Jack he was fired. The moment was becoming a perfect storm for disaster, and Mr. Brawley needed to get out now, or else he was going to need an extended visit to the bathroom.

Kasey and Herbert were coming up the driveway as the Brawleys were backing out, and it's a good thing they were paying attention so as to jump out of the way. The screeching of Mr. Brawley's tires as he took off down the street was enough to tell Herbert the meeting had not gone as well as expected. He went around the house, then snuck through the kitchen to his room to let Pierre out.

Unfortunately, Pierre was nowhere to be found. He was not in the house, unless he was in Jack's office, and Herbert had no plans to go in there. Pierre was not in the backyard, not under the pool, and didn't answer in the garage.

"He's over here," Kasey called from the break in the hedge. It seemed that Pierre had figured out a way to float out of the house, through the fence, and make his way into Kasey's backyard, where an attractive and energetic French poodle had been waiting for him.

"Well, at least we know the meeting wasn't ruined by Pierre, but I bet those other ghosts are in some way responsible."

Jack was surprisingly sweet about the whole thing with Mellissa. He opened the door and Mellissa carried a tray of glasses and bowls back to the kitchen. "Are you sure you're all right, Jack?"

"Some clients are not right for us," he said calmly and closed the door.

When the double doors to the office were closed and locked, and Mellissa was safely back in the kitchen, Jack became a caged lion in his own space. He yelled out to the air, he was certain that there were ghosts looking at him, laughing at him, and he was going to give them all that they were due. "Get out here, cowards. Dead blue cowardly spirits, I am not afraid of you, I'm not even the least bit afraid." Jack picked up a three-foot-long metal ruler and wielded it like a sword. "A ghost slicer, here it is. Appear and you'll see the wrath of my ruler." He checked closets, grasped at the air, and used the ruler to slice his beautiful ink drawings in half as they still hung on the wall. They drooped, shreds of paper still hanging by their tack pins. He took aim at the model, so much work, such a waste of time. "I am going to get exterminators, spiritualists, purifiers, supernatural cleaning experts, whatever it takes. Get ready because you guys are headed for the trash bins, you're going to be set out on the curb, you're going to be dead." He thought about it. "You're already dead, but you don't know dead like this. The fun is over, dead is nothing like you know dead to be now!" He raised his metal ruler, ready to bring it down and split the model in half like a grilled chicken. The blue ghost hand of Fabien reached out at the last second, and in midair stopped the ruler from damaging the model. Jack froze, and the phone rang.

"Hello?"

"Jack, it's the Brawleys."

"Yes."

"We're thinking maybe we overreacted. You know I have a sensitive stomach. But I don't want Mellissa to think I didn't appreciate all the work that went into that lovely jambalaya."

"No, no that's not a problem. The amount of work has us really swamped around here, that's all."

"Well, we wanted to come back by if you don't mind."

"Now?" Jacked looked around at the sliced-up drawings and general disarray he'd caused in the office. "Actually, I have another client about to arrive."

"Oh, well..."

"I have an idea." Jack was desperate not to miss an opening. "How about Friday evening? How about a barbecue? Let's have a little time to talk outside the project. I make an adventurous, I mean a *distinctive* rib eye and, trust me, it has no spice on it."

Jack listened. Mr. Brawley had covered the phone, and Jack could hear him conferring with Mrs. Brawley. Something told him there was another architect involved, as he distinctly heard, "That guy is even more of a lunatic than

Jack is..."

"Rib eye, corn, and potato salad, out by the pool." Casual, middle of the road, Jack was going in for the kill. The pool barbecue always worked.

Mr. Brawley sighed. "Friday evening it is, then."

As Mellissa cleaned the dishes and put the jambalaya into Tupperware, she noticed an uncapped bottle of Tabasco sauce on the counter. It was empty. "You monsters," she said, looking at the air.

As mad as she was, she just couldn't keep from laughing.

Until that is, her phone rang, too.

It was a surprise call from the vice principal at Herbert's school, and he called to say he was concerned that Herbert had missed school three days in a row. "This isn't normal for Herbert. Is there anything unusual going on?"

Mellissa tried to think, but other than a ghost dog, an unsuccessful séance, and two French-speaking ghosts who like to swim in the pool, help her in the kitchen, and sabotage client meetings, she couldn't think of a thing.

Now, most families at this time had something that would really act as a deterrent to misbehaving, the ultimate threat, the nuclear option, "Just wait until your father comes home." But in Herbert's case, his father was *always* home, so Mellissa had no such sword of Damocles to dangle above Herbert's head. Besides, she could hear rumblings from behind the closed doors of Jack's studio that suggested this latest bit of news might want to be Herbert's and her little secret. Still, she couldn't wait for him to get home, so she could drag out of him where the heck he had been spending the last three days and make it clear to him that *tomorrow* he would be spending his hours back in school.

Kasey walked Herbert and the dogs to the break in the hedge. "We didn't solve everything, but we had a pretty productive day together, don't you think, Herbert?"

It was an awkward moment, but Herbert was realizing that Kasey had become his true confidante; she was strategic, bold, an audacious ally, and he never would have gotten this far without her. He didn't know quite how to thank her.

She accepted his pause as progress. "Anyway, our dogs sure like each other."

Pierre broke the moment. He shuffled up, pushed Princess away, and fell down on the ground at Herbert's feet. He barely moved.

Herbert leaned down. "Something is wrong with him."

"What's he doing?" Kasey could only see the flattened grass where Pierre was probably laying. "Maybe he's just tired. He and Princess were probably running all afternoon."

But Herbert had never seen the dog this tired. He picked Pierre up in his arms. The characteristic blue flash in the dog's eyes was fading, going in and out from blue to a faded gray.

"I better get him home."

"See you at the bus tomorrow."

It was going to be a rough night for Herbert. He was going to get just a few sentences into his made-up story about how school had gone that day. Then, after just one intoxicatingly delicious bite of his mother's sausage, chicken, and frozen shrimp jambalaya, he was busted. The rest of the bowl was tossed in the trash, and he and Pierre were delivered back into his room. The door was to remain open, and so were the textbooks for the first time in three days. And not even Pierre got to lap up the leftover jambalaya. The rest of the night Herbert kept his eye on Pierre, who seemed just not to be himself.

Across the grass, on the other side of the driveway, Kasey was also grounded based on a similar phone call. Luckily, her parents didn't connect her uncharacteristic truancy with the boy next door, who didn't seem to pay any attention to her anyway, and so their command center in the back of the garage remained undiscovered and secure.

For all the drama that had played out, there was another person who ended up having a bad day. Late that night, Mr. Grimsley sat on a park bench in the nearly empty New Orleans Square at Disneyland. He looked across the river as the white riverboat paddled into its dock to moor for the night. This was usually a moment of inspiration for him. But tonight, he looked weary. His tie was loosened and his name tag was hidden away in his pocket. He had bought the last box of popcorn but had snacked on only a few kernels. A pigeon landed next to him, took a few bites, and he barely noticed. He checked his watch, stood up, and headed toward the exit of the Haunted Mansion.

Down the exit, the music and voices had ceased for today's previews. The few cast members were clearing out. He slipped into the door marked CONSTRUCTION ONLY. With everything quiet he entered the ride building; he took a small flashlight, but he barely

needed it. He knew every step of his way, every character, every prop, every shadow, and every cobblestone on the ground. He worked his way, stepping carefully out through the attic, past the now static undertaker and his dog, through the iron gates and into the vast expanse of the graveyard scene. He looked across the tombstones and out toward the farthest scene, the troubadours. The pair of guys with the timpani drums were still there. The bagpiper was still there.

But the soldier, the trumpeter, and the howling dog had all disappeared.

Chapter 12

Back to School

When the bus driver opened the door that morning, he was surprised to find not just Kasey and Herbert, but also two sets of stern parents, all in bathrobes. Kasey and Herbert stepped up onto the bus like they were headed for prison. The doors closed, they took their seats, and they tried their best not to make eye contact with the concerned parents looking up at them from the sidewalk.

"What did you have?" Kasey asked as they cleared

the view of the prison guards.

"Stomach flu," Herbert read off a note, "projectile vomiting, perhaps motivated by a shellfish allergy. I added that part."

"Wow, creative." Kaley was impressed and compared her note. "I should have spent more time on it, we just went with 102-degree fever, chills, and a concern for possible delirium."

"Still works."

"I'm feeling much, much, better."

"Yeah, but he's not." Herbert looked into the top of his backpack, where Pierre was settled in, half asleep.

"What's he doing?" Kasey tried to see in the bag, but all she saw was billowing canvas.

"Nothing, that's the problem. A ghost dog that's suddenly got no energy, I guess it's a bad sign."

"Maybe the Yellow Pages has a listing for a ghost dog veterinarian." She quieted down, realizing others were probably listening, and it was a bad joke anyway. "I don't think a dog can die twice, Herbie." She thought about it and wondered if that was necessarily true.

Kasey's mother and Mellissa weren't really friends but sometimes you needed to confer with the next-door neighbor, especially when truancy was involved. This took the form of a serious conference, in bathrobes, coffee cups in hand, through the gap in the hedge.

"I hope they're not, you know." Kasey's mom was quite concerned.

"Oh no, Herbert, oh no, not even close. I mean, nothing I've seen would even suggest that."

"We'd be the last to know."

"Herbert's got some depression issues right now. Not major, just the dog."

"Kasey told me you've got a new dog. That helps, I hope."

"Well, sort of a dog, I guess."

"Sort of a dog?"

"Just trying it out."

"Do you have a lot of parties?"

"No, oh, no, not parties, Jack's clients come over sometimes."

"Didn't sound like client meetings to us, yelling, screeching tires. And do you have to use the pool so late at night? Sometimes it wakes us up when you guys are cannonballing after eleven o'clock."

"We'll try to be quieter. I've got to go let that dog out."

"That sort of a dog?"

"That one, even a sort of a dog has to go out once in a while." Mellissa slinked away. She felt like she was running a terrible household, a flophouse with her son disappearing in the daytime with the neighbor girl, and pool parties to all hours of the night.

"The neighbors are getting suspicious." She sat across the big table from Jack.

"We better keep Herbert home and the dog inside."

"Keep the backyard quiet."

"I've got a barbecue tomorrow." Jack started to worry. He whispered, "Maybe I should drain the pool to keep those guys out of it." He thought about it. "Nah, that would look pretty ugly."

"We've got another problem," Mellissa whispered too. "I don't know where the dog is."

Pierre didn't seem to like the math teacher any more than Herbert did. The ghost dog had revived a little, at least enough to be struggling against the backpack and wanting to get out and stretch. Herbert brought his pack around and started to open the flap. He realized he was in eye contact with Truck, the menace was practically in his face.

"You going to throw up in your backpack?"

"I'll probably have to because I filled yours up already." Herbert didn't have any spare time to waste on this jerk anymore.

Truck checked his pack just in case Herbert wasn't kidding.

"Hey." Truck could be counted on to not make quiet small talk for very long. "Herbert's going to hurl one and he's trying to use my backpack!"

Truck set off a major in-room ruckus. Students near Herbert jumped away, and the math teacher panicked at the thought of having to get out the bag of green vomit dust, and a full pack of paper towels. No one but Herbert saw the ghost dog jump out of the backpack, run across Herbert's desk, over Truck's desk, and dive desk over desk, forming a phantom gust of wind that threw students' papers everywhere.

The teacher led Herbert and Truck quickly by the shoulders out into the hall. She steered Herbert toward the boys' room, and kept Truck moving down the corridor, off to visit the vice principal for another typical mid-class outburst.

Herbert snuck back out and hunted for Pierre. He finally found him, settled and panting in one corner of the grassy quad. The poor dog could only move at half his normal speed as if his legs were asleep and he couldn't control them properly. He got Pierre some water from the fountain and settled him back inside the backpack, just in time for the bell, and the flood of students headed for their next class.

That familiar feeling of dread came over Herbert, as he realized it was third period. He had missed three days of basketball practice, and if Truck got out of the vice principal's office in time, he'd be a major pain after their vomitous altercation.

Herbert reached up and set his backpack with Pierre inside on a mid-level gym bleacher. He circled his arms, getting ready to play. He felt different like he'd bulked up a little, and he didn't feel quite so weak in his basketball uniform. Maybe all that keeping up with Pierre was doing something good for him. He entered the dreaded team-picking exercise with slightly more confidence. Truck returned just in time too.

Herbert played his best, and his best was better than

his normal. He was confidently headed for a layup shot, but Truck fouled him, just before he could shoot. Coach Dale whistled to stop but didn't call out Truck. Herbert dribbled again, trying to move toward the basket, but Truck was all over him. Herbert turned around and tried to go around him, but Truck was locked on him. Herbert turned, and out of frustration, he tried an impossibly stupid mid-court shot. The ball hit the rim and arched way out over the bleachers, hitting Herbert's backpack from the side. The pack teetered on the edge for a second and rolled over the edge to fall, with Pierre locked inside. Herbert tried to run for it, but it was impossible to get there. He watched as the pack fell, and just as it was about to slam onto the court, it magically slowed down, as if it had been plucked out of thin air, and it swung, landing safely into Herbert's arms.

The brutal battle continued. Herbert intercepted a pass intended for Truck. Truck came right at him. Herbert felt the ball spin in his hands, and he wasn't controlling it. It ramped up to such a high spin that blue smoke started forming around it. Herbert's hands got so hot he passed the ball to a teammate. It was too hot for him too, so he tossed the spinning ball, now trailing blue smoke like a comet, to someone else.

Finally, another teammate passed it across the court and Truck dove in to intercept it. Truck received the full brunt of the ball to the stomach, and it was so intense it took him off his feet and threw him off the court where he crashed into a laundry bin full of dirty towels. Now Truck was angry. Coach Dale whistled and Truck was back on the court, doing his best to manage the strange ball. Herbert came up to him, and without doing anything, the ball jumped from Truck's dribble over to Herbert. Herbert moved toward the basket, but Truck drove right over him. They collided, both hit the floor hard, and rolled right out of the court. Coach Dale finally called a foul.

Herbert moved to the free throw line, and someone passed him the ball. He looked at the strange ball, bounced it, and spun it around. He looked up at the basket, knowing full well he'd never make the shot. The ball was slippery, and he had trouble just keeping it from sliding out of his grip.

"Hey, Herbert, you going to shoot that?" Coach Dale was trying to figure out what was taking Herbert so much time. The coach came up and said privately to Herbert, "What's the problem, Herbie? You going to let that blowhard Truck bother you, son? You just get up there and shoot that ball."

The other players started sassing him, but Herbert tried to shut it all out. Then he saw them, two blue eyes appeared out of the mist, staring out from the ball, and giggling at him. He wound

down, bent his knees, and sprang up. The ball arched high but not high enough; it looked like it would not even make it to the rim.

As in any accident, had it been possible to slow that one key moment down, it would have been clear to everyone what happened. As it was, everybody saw something different. The coach had seen the trajectory of the ball as it left Herbert's hands and knew absolutely that it wouldn't make it to the rim. He looked down at the ground, took off his hat, and mouthed "damn." Herbert's team looked down in more or less unison as they knew they were missing an important point. Truck's team's faces turned upward, and they raised their hands and started to jump up off the court.

From Herbert's angle, he saw himself come down

with just enough knee bend, then he lifted the ball with his upper body, letting it go with no snap but a slight backspin as it left his hands. He could tell it was going to be short. That's when he realized the distinctive blue head of the ghost soldier was somehow inside the ball, laughing and spinning.

By turning faster, he lifted the trajectory, perfectly placing the ball, or ghost head, or ghost ball, whatever you'd call it on the backboard, and with a small rotation, right into the basket. Coach Dale's eyes lifted as he realized Herbert had somehow made the shot, and he smiled. Truck's face sank from whooping, smug delight, to something that looked more like the backside of a chicken.

Over the sound of his team roaring, Herbert heard the distinctive cackling of ghosts, and Pierre's muffled barking from inside the backpack too.

The celebration continued later on the bus, Herbert's teammates high-fiving him as he jumped on and ran back to the seat next to Kasey. She got the idea from all the yelling that Herbert had somehow been the star player at the game.

Herbert whispered, "I had a few assists."

From inside the backpack, Pierre was rolling around, trying to catch a sniff of whatever the excitement was all about.

Kasey smiled, as she just wanted Herbert to have this moment. She looked at him differently—he looked stronger, kind of self-confident. He leaned his head back and looked directly into her eyes. She couldn't remember him ever doing that before.

Chapter 13

A Magical Evening

That beautiful ready-to-cook charcoal smell wafted by Herbert and Kasey as they stepped out of the bus and parted. A little wave was all they had because they were still grounded, and neither of them could imagine a way they'd have another chance to sneak off to their command center, not for a while, anyway.

Herbert was overjoyed to learn that he was not required at the client's dinner. He was happy to let Pierre have a few moments' spin and a few sniffs around the now immaculate backyard, and they were off to Herbert's room for an evening of homework and Salisbury steak. But Pierre seemed less enthusiastic. In fact, it took him longer than normal to wet a couple of trees and a plant for good measure. He stopped several times just to lie down and pant. Herbert worried maybe he had spent too much time cooped up in the backpack all day.

Mellissa was in luck, there was one Swanson Salisbury steak TV dinner left in the back of the freezer, and she slid it into the oven. The "twice-baked" potatoes were on their second cycle in the oven. The Caesar salad had the exact combination of mayonnaise, croutons, parmesan, and the anchovies, which just swam through the Worcestershire sauce but didn't stay. She even tried not to flinch, or reveal any lack of confidence when Jack said, "Something interesting for dessert?"

Something interesting for dessert sounds easy to someone who tosses a steak and some salt on the coals and throws the butcher paper in the garbage. Something interesting likely didn't include Jell-O, ice cream, or a chocolate chip cookie. She desperately called out to her ghost chefs but there was no response. She even tried her high school French, "*Maintenant serait le moment ideal.*" But there was not a pâtissier to be found.

If Herbert and his dad could have turned their backyard into a compact Adventureland, they would have. They came close—the stained-wood decks, thatched canopies, and the deep green tropical planting had been inspired by the original. Recognizing the gravity of this particular evening, Jack had even opted to light the torches. Their kerosene flames brought magic to the setting, and an added golden flicker to the freshly trimmed birds of paradise. Somehow good food, served under the stars, was working, not in a high-pressure sales kind of way, but in a natural, mutual, storytelling way that was how Jack liked to work anyway. The Brawleys had found Jack's hard-line black-and-white drawings cold, boring, and lacking in understanding of two people who'd spent years together, and just wanted a special place to have their kids and grandkids over for holidays.

One thing Jack rarely revealed to clients was his passion for sketching, preferably on a thick stack of paper napkins. When the pen met the soft paper, it was like paint to fresco. Jack feared the informality, because a sketch was a channel to his heart, with no accounts payable, no measurements and specifications getting in the way. On those rare occasions when he did uncap his fountain pen, his sketches became an intimate connection between mind, soul, experience, and his hand, and in the case of the Brawleys that night, they felt it. Jack was not too adventuresome; they had just lost their sense of adventure. Maybe a new house for them was not about new walls and floors, but something to define *their* next adventure.

Mr. Brawley mustered up what for him was a very positive comment. "Jack, you're all right."

Throwing a rock up to the second-floor window is hard. It's even harder holding a sleeping dog in your arms. But Herbert tried anyway. Nothing happened. He tried another one, a little bigger.

"You're going to break my window!" Kasey appeared, right behind Herbert, and scared him out of his skin. "I heard the first one!" She looked up at her parents' bedroom window. "I think they're asleep, but they'll kill me if we go in the garage."

Herbert held up Pierre. Although she couldn't see him, she could tell from Herbert's face that something was terribly wrong.

"I need to find out what to do if he's sick."

Kasey knew it was worse than that. Herbert wanted to know if his ghost dog could die a second time.

"Come on." She led him quietly into the garage through the side door.

A Magical Evening

Mellissa set the dishes down on the counter and looked around. "Darn!" She had half expected she'd walk into freshly baked beignets and coffee again. But there was nothing.

"Mellissa, dear, you're kidding!" Mrs. Brawley was headed back outside and stopped in the dining room. "These are amazing!"

"Oh, thank you," Mellissa played dumb and took a look at the cut-crystal cups sitting on the table.

"And so fancy!"

Mellissa didn't see fancy, she saw pastry cups with a sort of wilted banana mix lying in them, with a bit of ice cream in the center. Her ghost team, she thought, was slacking off. *Where are they?*

"I'm going back outside; I can't wait to see the excitement!"

Mellissa was lost. *What excitement?*

"Bananas flambé!"

Mellissa was learning that Jérôme and Fabien dropped in when they felt like it. *"Flambé est magnifique!"* They were clearly excited about this culinary adventure as they loaded her up with the tray. Then Fabien tried to open a bottle. He looked a little weak and couldn't. He handed it to Jérôme, who didn't have the strength, either. Mellissa set the tray down and opened the bottle, surprised that the cork slipped out so easily.

They offered Mellissa a smell from the bottle, and it nearly knocked her down. Whatever it was, it came from somewhere where they knew how to make it. Jérôme did the honors, pouring way too much on each dessert. Then they handed a match to Mellissa.

"Feux d'artifice ils vont adorer!"

Whatever that meant, she could tell from Fabien and Jérôme's hand motions it probably meant fireworks.

In the dim light of their garage control center, Kasey read to Herbert quietly from the *Ghost World* book. In fact, she already knew the passages that were relevant to Herbert's concern. She was just trying to decide if she'd really read them to him or try to shield her best friend from the bad news.

"He just lost all of his energy."

"The good news is, ghosts don't die, you don't do that twice."

"Well, that's encouraging."

"That's the good news. You want to hear the rest of it?"

"Read it."

"It says here that ghosts don't always stay where they are first discovered. 'They have been known to follow the people they love to other places. They have also been known to be eliminated by certain rituals or magical séances.' I guess at some point ghosts just..." She stopped.

Herbert took the book and found the place. "let me read it, 'at some point, ghosts just fade away. They don't die twice, but their presence just slips away, and they may never be heard from again,' *never heard from again.*"

Herbert handed the book back to Kasey, and she closed it. He cradled the quiet dog in his lap.

Kasey came up and tried to feel the dog too. "You know I've never even seen him."

"I know, I wish you could. He's really a good dog."

"There's something else," she said, and she opened the book again. "Transference." She had trouble finding it, and shined a flashlight across her boards, finding the note card she was looking for. "If a ghost appears to someone they loved, someone else *that* person loves, may sometimes also see the same ghost."

"Which is why my parents can see them all now."

"Well, maybe if he thinks we like each other, I could see him too."

"How could the dog know if I like you?"

"As far as he can see, we just argue all the time." Kasey looked a little unhappy about it.

"Pierre, I like Kasey, can you show yourself to her?" Pierre looked up but didn't seem interested in doing any appearances at the moment.

"Maybe try a little stronger statement?" Kasey knew dogs weren't exactly famous for their subtlety.

"Pierre, I like Kasey."

And there was a long pause before Herbert spoke again.

"Actually, I more than like her."

As far as Kasey could tell, Herbert's great reveal did nothing.

But she had one more idea. "Is he looking at you?"

"Yes, he is. His blue eyes are looking right at me."

Kasey moved in close. "Okay, in the interest of science!" She put her lips against Herbert's. It started as a little peck, but somewhere between the two of them, it evolved quickly into what years later would be remembered as a pretty darn good first kiss. Without interrupting, she strained her eyes down toward where the dog was, and then suddenly she broke away.

"I see him!"

And she did. Pierre rolled over slightly. "He rolled over. I see him!"

She picked up the dog and balanced him in her arms, then she leaned back and rested her head on Herbert's shoulder.

On the backyard table, Mellissa set the tray down and got ready to strike the match. It wouldn't strike, and finally, the head snapped off.

"Let me help you, Mel," Mr. Brawley was really connected now. He took out a lighter. "There she blows!"

Had anyone at that table taken a culinary class, they would know that a flambé can be a dramatic culmination to a wonderful meal, but certain safety rules best be observed. It's best to use a long fireplace match. Always ignite the fumes at the edge of the pan and not in the liquid itself. Never lean over the dish or pan, as you light the fumes. The last note is where Mr. Brawley had misjudged. The flambé was, in fact, *magnifique*, everyone agreed and applauded. And at his age, Mr. Brawley's eyebrows grew back quickly, anyway. Seeing success, Jérôme and Fabien decided on a ceremonial cannonball into the pool.

"What the heck was that?" Mr. Brawley wondered, finishing his last banana.

"Sprinklers," Jack tried, matter-of-fact.

"Sprinklers, my keister. Someone just jumped in your pool."

"Kids, they love to swim at all hours."

Kasey's parents had the lights on and were already trying to see what idiots were in the neighbors' pool at this hour. As they looked down, they saw something worse than the late-night swim. They realized there was a dim light and some movement in the back of their garage.

Mr. Brawley seemed intent to know who had decided to take a swim in the middle of *his* honorary barbecue, and

Jack was equally intent on not letting him go up the steps to the deck. Mr. Brawley probably wouldn't have cared that much, except Jack seemed so intent on hiding it. They had a polite tussle, and it got a little more heated when Mrs. Brawley stepped into the light.

"Dear," she said, "your eyebrows are gone."

Despite the loud sounds next door, Kasey's parents tried to keep silent as they crept down the stairs, out the back door, and toward the side door of their dimly lit garage.

Kasey's father reached in slowly to open the side door. He picked up an iron rake and held it up threateningly. The light was coming from a crack behind the boat. He pressed on the improvised wall, which collapsed in on itself. What they discovered was worse than any prowler or raccoon family would have been. A secret room packed full of papers, books, display boards, and a model, and in the center their daughter, late at night, sitting way too close to the boy next door.

The swimming pool standoff was about to end. Mr. Brawley was inclined to back off and try to make the best of an otherwise good evening, and things might have ended tense but positive. But something else unexpected was about to happen. From the neighbors' side of the driveway, two people wearing pajamas and unmatched slippers appeared. Kasey's mom held an iron rake, and Kasey was trying to hide behind her. Kasey's father pushed a wheelbarrow into the middle of Jack's yard and used the rake to empty all of the contents out onto the dichondra lawn.

"What is this?" Jack inquired.

"You should know, it's all yours. Models, drawings, boards, it all came out of your office."

"My office, nothing came out of my office."

"Well, ask your son about it."

"My son, what's he have to do with it? He's sleeping in his room."

"Well, you better check on him, because if I ever catch him in our garage with our daughter again, I'll call the cops. And tell him to stop filling Kasey's head with crazy stories about ghosts, and transference, and whatever else all this stuff is about."

In Jack's driveway, the Brawleys had managed to slip away from the confrontation. Their car started as Mrs. Brawley was still running toward the passenger door. She jumped in. Jack stepped over the pile of model parts and papers to run after them, dragging bits of paper and cardboard along under his feet. He ran after the car, trying to get Mr. Brawley to stop. Mr. Brawley screeched his tires and took off, spinning Jack down onto the street.

In the backyard, the neighbors had taken their wheelbarrow, and their rake, and their daughter, and gone home. Jack stood confused, looking at the pile of model pieces and research boards.

Mellissa came out of the door. "He's not here, Jack!" Herbert was not sleeping as she thought he was.

"Where the heck is he?"

Pierre barked from up on the pool deck.

"Help, help him!" It was Herbert's voice.

Herbert was safe and dry, but terrified. Pierre was barking but unable to get up, just sitting on his legs, panting.

Standing next to him was the blue glowing Jérôme, shivering,

"Mon Dieu! le sauve, il se noie!"

"My God, he's drowning. We've got to save him," Mellissa could barely make out Fabien, at the bottom of the pool, a dim flickering blue light.

Jack stood back. "He can't drown, he's a ghost and not a very helpful one."

"Quelqu'un fait quelque chose!"

"We have to do something!" Herbert yelled helplessly.

Mellissa had seen enough. She kicked off her shoes and

jumped into the pool, with all of her clothes on. She managed to swim to the bottom, wrapped her arms around Fabien, and pulled him up. They laid him on the deck, where Jérôme and Herbert turned him over, ejecting pool water from inside his glowing form.

Fabien finally sat up and they covered him with a towel. He looked at Mellissa, shivering in her soaked clothes. *"Comment était la flambé, tout le monde en a-t-il apprécié?"*

Mellissa laughed. "Yes, they loved the bananas flambé," she said, dripping from pool water or tears, it was hard to tell. She looked at Jack, hoping to see a little compassion from the husband and father, from the man she trusted so much.

"I just don't believe any of this is happening, but if it's real, I want it to go away." Jack started down the deck steps. Car lights lit them all for a moment, as a car pulled up to the front of the house.

"The Brawleys, they changed their mind again." Jack looked at Mellissa, soaked.

"Oh, Jack, forget them. There are more important things." She looked down at Herbert, who was holding the dog, and the two shivering ghosts.

"You and Herbert can lose your minds or live in an imaginary world where you can accept hysterical illusion,

but one of us has to keep it together." Jack stormed for the back door. "Somebody has to keep a roof over our heads." He slammed the door as he went in. Mellissa and Herbert watched as he stood in the kitchen taking a deep breath, and then he headed to the front door.

Jack opened the front door, his client smile plastered back on, and then his expression changed. "Just who the hell are you?"

"I thought you'd know. I'm sorry if it's too late." On the porch, looking ghostly gray in the yellow bug light, was Grimsley. "I thought maybe your son told you about me."

"My son?" Jack looked up and down the street, stepped out on the porch, and closed the door behind him. "Oh yes, of course, my son told me about you. But you know what, we're all full up. We've got all the ghosts we can handle at the moment. Maybe you should check in next door. They might love to have their own ghost over there."

"But I, uh." Grimsley was confused, to say the least.

"Oh, not fun enough for you, I know you all like to just have a good time, like this." Jack reached out and grabbed hold of Grimsley's head, turned it from side to side, and tried to pull it off his shoulders.

"Hey, that hurts!"

"Oh, come on, we love this game, a little ball game." Slowly, Jack started to realize Grimsley's head was not going to pop off as readily as Jérôme's and Fabien's would. He reared back and thrust his fist toward Grimsley's chest, but to his surprise, his arm didn't just pass through him as he thought it should. Instead, poor Grimsley fell back on the stairs. Jack caught him and steadied him. "Not a ghost, huh?

"Not yet."

Jack looked at Grimsley suspiciously. "Ah, sorry."

Had the Beatles or Elvis come into the backyard at that moment, they would have gotten the same reception. As soon as Grimsley stepped out the back door, Pierre, who'd been lying around all day, rallied, jumped up, and ran toward Grimsley, dove up at him, passed through him, then dove in and through from the other side, barking all the time.

"I told you never to do that," Grimsley said, trying to shake the dog off.

When Jérôme and Fabien heard the ruckus, they ran toward Grimsley, hugging him and slapping him on the back, their slaps running right through him also. He put his hands up and tried to free himself from the circle of blue invasion.

The ghosts all settled down for a moment.

"So, it turns out you're just a liar," said Herbert.

"Herbert!" Mellissa was shocked.

"No, he's right, I guess I am. I am just a big liar. But I really didn't set out to be one." He sat down next to Herbert. Pierre curled up at Grimsley's feet.

Chapter 14

Grimsley Comes Clean

"Over the years, I guess, I've just come to be the ghost guy. These two, Herbert and your neighbor, Kasey, I guess it was, you were pretty brave coming to see me. And I owe you an apology. I didn't come clean then, but I guess I will now. I tried to tell this story so many times. Since no one was ever going to believe me, I just stopped believing it myself."

"How do you know him?" Mellissa was trying to

figure out how her son knew this man.

"Well, I guess you don't remember, and I'm not that memorable, but the first time we met was that night at the Haunted Mansion, the night Herbert first got disoriented."

"So, you knew about it." Jack started to put the pieces together. "All the time."

"I traveled across the country for a couple of years, just studying ghosts, obsessed with them. I think I went to half the haunted houses along the eastern seaboard, then down across the south. I looked for Revolutionary War ghosts, pioneer ghosts, and just plain old creaky apparitions in odd people's attics. One thing I learned for sure, and I meant it when I told you, Herbert, most ghost stories are just that, stories. They're made up by towns who want more tourists, by people who love to make up tragic tales, and by the folks who want to read them, and by some people who are just so lonely, they can't let go of someone they love. Some folks just have something unresolved, deep inside of them, and having a ghost around is the only way they can deal with it."

"These guys all seem pretty real to me." Mellissa looked around, one big happy supernatural family.

"There were some stories that just couldn't be explained away by science or magic, or publicity. A few that just proved that there was something to all this ghost legend stuff, maybe not all of it, but here and there. Oh yeah, and there were a few who kept following me. This little dog, Pierre, you called him, yes, he's been with me a long time. There was a cat too, and an old lady, but she got tired of picking up after me. I thought I had a ghost in the laundry room until I realized the sound was coming from a leaky water heater. But these guys, they're a piece of work. I guess you found that out. But they cook pretty good if you like it spicy."

"Where did you find them?"

"I'd say they found me. In an old house, the Beauregard House, and they just followed me. I tried to get them to go back, but they just latched on to me. Eventually, I said, 'You go earn your keep in the mansion.' By that time, I'd had enough ghost hunting for a lifetime."

"How do we get rid of them?" Jack returned to the practical matter.

"Eventually they're going to fade away." He looked down at Pierre. "Looks like this little guy is already on his way."

Herbert said, "But what if we don't want them to die, what if they're our friends?"

"Oh, they don't die," Grimsley said, "they already did that. If they're out in the world, like these guys are, away from the source of their energy, away from their history and their memories, they will eventually just fade away. You'll just wake up one day, and you won't remember they were ever here.

"But what if we don't want that?" Mellissa clearly didn't. "What if we don't like the whole idea of some made-up 'better place,' or any of that? What if we think we have a better place for them?"

"Please, Mr. Grimsley," Herbert said, "I don't want them to fade away. We've got enough people and friends in life that fade away. Why can't we just have a few that we can hold on to?"

"Well, I don't know exactly, but I do have a theory."

"Now we're getting somewhere." Mellissa looked hopeful.

Jérôme and Fabien mustered up coffee and whipped up a few biscotti.

"This is decaf, right?" Grimsley asked before he took a sip.

"N'est bien, sur!"

"See?" Grimsley had a sip, looked around the group,

and continued. "It's not just my theory, it's been around for a while. You can't keep them with you—here, I mean. But if you want to keep them in your hearts, your memories, you've got to get them back, back to where they started, to their origin point."

Jack interrupted. "You mean Disneyland? I don't think they're going to let us back in there again!"

Grimsley laughed, and looked from Herbert to Mellissa, and back again.

"No, the origin point for Jérôme and Fabien, and Pierre, or whatever names they really have, is an old, abandoned mansion in New Orleans."

"New Orleans?"

Jack looked at Herbert. Pierre rested comfortably in his arms, as Napoleon had, for so many years as his son was growing up. He searched Mellissa's eyes for some bit of logic, something that would say this will all be a bunch of bunk when we wake up tomorrow. But Mellissa didn't have that look for Jack, what Mellissa had for Jack was the love she first had and always had for him. The love for the guy who believed in things, who believed in imagination, and adventure, and magic. And the guy who now had a son and a wife, who believed in him.

"I'm going to go there. I'll take the bus if I have to," Herbert said.

"That's a long ride," said Grimsley.

"I don't care. I'm not going to just sit here and watch them just fade away."

As he was known to do sometimes, Jack fell out of the conversation. On Jack's mind at that moment was one of the reasons he had used to justify buying the Ford Country Squire. He took a mental count of the wagon's passenger capacity: with two seats across the front, three across the back, and the bonus rear seat that could comfortably seat a few too, he could comfortably accommodate six and the dog.

"Jack, what are you thinking about?" Mellissa asked.

Jack didn't answer. Jack was thinking about a road trip.

Chapter 15

Road to New Orleans

After one long day of intense planning, the garage door automatically opened at five o'clock in the morning, the vacuum headlights on the wagon started to glow, and the spotless polished red, wood-sided car emerged, efficiently loaded, with a new matching Coleman ice chest strapped to the top rack, and small pillows and blankets distributed around the three compartments. Mr. Grimsley had returned freshly armed with a satchel holding his research, a map, his leather-bound sketchbook and pencils, and his ultracompact Remington electric razor.

It took only a few minutes to get everyone loaded. Jack and Mellissa took command up front, with Jack's special spot for his coffee travel mug that no one dared touch. Mellissa was armed with the most important navigation device ever invented, the Automobile Association TripTik, freshly printed and spiral bound at the top, its information deeply personalized and up to date as of yesterday afternoon.

Grimsley was none too pleased to be crowded in the second seat, with two ghosts for whom seat belts weren't necessary, and besides, they had no sense of personal space. Jérôme and Fabien were excited to explore this amazing, modern American automobile, or *voiture de luxe,* as they called it, speaking bits of French to each other, while popping on and off the dome lights, opening and closing the electric windows, and flipping up and down those little metal lids on the in-door ashtrays.

Kasey snuck through the fence and met Herbert before he closed the rear door. She gave Pierre a few scratches behind his glowing floppy ears.

"I wish I could go with you."

"Yeah."

"Do you wish I could go with you?"

"Sure."

"Really?"

"I think so."

Considering their shared journey up to now, Kasey had hoped to hear a little more enthusiasm. So when her mom called from the other side of the fence, she realized there was really nothing left for her to say. She got out and started back toward her house. Herbert watched her, and she didn't look back.

Jack couldn't help observing from the front seat. "Herbert, sometimes there is a moment, a moment when you know the right thing to do. Now, I'm no expert, but I think this might be a time you want to go after her."

Herbert grabbed Pierre, and indeed, ran after her. He bolted through the fence and took his chance. He blurted it all out at once to Kasey's mom. "We're going to New Orleans because we have to take the ghosts back so they can live on and still be in our hearts."

She looked at him like he had sadly lost his mind. The boy with the imaginary dog cradled in his arms and the strange group of adults preparing for some kind of trip made her want to call Family Services.

"I can't do it without her," he finally said.

Kasey went for broke. "Can I go with them?" She already knew the answer, but the question came out anyway. Her mom took her by the arm and started to lead her inside.

"Wait, he's real, I can prove it to you!" Herbert suddenly knew he couldn't leave Kasey behind. He sat the dog on the ground at the feet of Kasey and her mom.

"This is Pierre, and Pierre loves me, and I love Pierre, and Kasey loves me…"

Kasey's mom looked even more worried; she folded her arms. "You *love* him?"

Kasey thought an explanation was appropriate. "It's probably just a youthful romance, which is an important contributor to adolescent self-understanding and identity formation, rather than true intimacy."

"I see."

"So, Pierre loves, me, and I love Pierre, and Kasey loves me, so she can see Pierre too."

"You see something?"

"I see a dog. He's so cute."

"So?"

"Pierre loves me, and I love Pierre."

"You're leaving out something." Kasey was folding her

arms now, too.

"Oh, Pierre loves me, and I love Pierre." Herbert slowed down and tried, "And I like Kasey, I more than like Kasey, maybe I love Kasey, and Kasey must love me, otherwise she couldn't see Pierre, and since you love Kasey, you can probably see Pierre, too."

"Show me, Mom."

"This is ridiculous."

"Mom!"

Her mom put an arm coldly around her.

"No, Mom. Down here and like you mean it."

Reluctantly, she came down on her knees in front of some kind of a phantom magic trick, and lovingly hugged her daughter. Then Kasey's mom broke into tears, hugged her again, brought her eyes down to the grass, and held her hand out. "Oh my God, he's really there!"

Yes, Kasey's mom had seen the blue dog too. The big lightning eyes melted her skeptical heart just enough for her to send Kasey upstairs to pack a small bag, get their Kodak Instamatic camera with one flash cube, and her math homework. As she tucked Herbert, Kasey, and the ghost dog safely into seats and closed the rear door, she said, "I have no idea how I can possibly explain this to your father."

According to the AAA TripTik, the trip to New Orleans was going to take twenty-six hours. This, of course, was drive time and didn't include stops. Jack was philosophically opposed to stopping for anything other than gas, clean bathrooms, and a collective snooze in a safe, well-lit rest area. A motel was not an option.

Jack knew deep in his heart you could make a vacation out of anything, especially if you had the right mindset. He knew from his brief trip to the Auto Club that morning that he could follow the Mother Road, the Main Street of America, historic Route 66, all the way to Amarillo, Texas, and without losing too much time, he could shoot back down to the gulf and meet up with I-10 to efficiently roll into New Orleans. Like all of Jack's design schemes, it was brilliant and imaginative, and a chance to break out of monotony. And like all of his schemes, he was about to create a lot of extra work for himself.

The first ninety minutes of the drive set the pace, and the lack of disagreements seemed to bode well for a perfect trip. Everyone was feeling good, and Mellissa suggested a quick breakfast stop would be the perfect booster rocket.

The counter at the diner in Cabazon had seven seats

open. Although there was no café au lait, Mellissa slid two cups of coffee with a splash of cream over to Jérôme and Fabien, who seemed content with that and a few slices of toast. Had the counter server not worked all night, it's likely she would have noticed coffee and toast being consumed into thin air by no one at two empty seats. She either didn't notice or working in an all-night diner in the desert had left her lacking in mental sensibility or responsiveness to just about anything.

Jack inhaled his high-protein sausage, bacon, and eggs breakfast, and left Mellissa to pay and manage the group, and headed out efficiently to top off the wagon's tank.

A cool desert wind passed through the parking lot; a few tumbleweeds rolled through. Jack's step slowed and he vectored toward the back of the parking lot as if something was drawing him there.

Standing before him was the most confusing structure he had ever seen. It was more than a hundred feet long, at least thirty feet wide, and organically fitted together by hand. A man was about two stories up, welding, with sparks falling down toward Jack's feet.

The man pushed back his welding helmet and looked down at Jack. "Well, you gonna just stare, or you wanna bring me up a pile of them rods?" Jack picked up some steel reinforcing bars, carried them up the improvised ladder and laid them at the man's feet.

"What is it?"

"Can't you tell?"

It would be a few more years before anyone could tell that old, wiry Claude K. Bell, in the middle of the desert, was hand-building a brontosaurus out of scrap steel and plaster, and years beyond that before anyone could tell whether or not he was crazy. But Jack recognized Claude's genius immediately. Like Jack, this was a craftsman of curved organic form, a purveyor of an adventurous vision.

"Where are your plans?"

"Plans? What the hell would I need plans for?"

"How do you know what you're building?"

"Ghosts."

"Ghosts?"

"The dinosaurs, they visit me at night, I hear them walking. I get out of bed, come out here, and I can see them, all laid out perfectly. Ten of them, all along here. The next morning, I know exactly where to start." He motioned to Jack, and Jack handed him a few more bars. From high above, Jack could see Mellissa herding everyone out of the restaurant.

"That your family?"

"Yes."

"Good thing you got a big car."

Jack wondered, *Is this guy just crazy, or can he see ghosts?* "It's pretty roomy when you only have five," Jack said.

"A little more crowded when you've got seven, eh? And room for a dog too."

Given the schedule, Jack decided not to pursue the notion further, and he started to move back to the ladder.

"Be careful on the road."

"Oh yeah," Jack smiled as he went down the ladder.

"Things can be dangerous."

Jack didn't really know what the old man meant, but he gave a wave anyway.

"Jack, look out," Mellissa yelled at Jack as he approached the car. A huge rusted semi-truck pulled out from behind, cut too close, and shaved off the wagon's right front fender, taking a few feet of shiny aluminum trim and the radio antenna with it. Jack ran alongside the driver trying to get his attention, but the guy was oblivious; he just left Jack standing in dust and diesel smoke, holding his broken antenna in his hand.

Not much was spoken for the next couple of hundred miles, and needless to say, the radio no longer worked. Mellissa studied the TripTik, and Grimsley doodled in his sketchbook, pushing the ghosts over when they tried to lean on him while snoring.

Herbert looked down at Kasey, who had fallen asleep on a pillow next to him. She suddenly looked like a wonder of nature to him. How could he never have noticed the neat way she wrapped her short hair behind her perfect ears, or how pink and clean and shaped her nails were? He looked at his own nails, dirty and chewed. There must be some genetic advantage. She was so smart, so pretty, and she somehow naturally exceeded all of his capabilities. He opened the back window a crack, and Pierre showed some energy, standing up so he could put his nose out into the moving air.

Grimsley looked at the dog, across to the ghosts, and up toward Jack and Mellissa. One thing he knew from his years making research trips was that silence wasn't fun, and without some excitement, even some conflict, there was no drama, no story, and without story, there would be no bonding of this ragtag group on their terribly long drive together. And some bonding, he knew, was going to be necessary to get through this adventure.

"I think we're near the Thing, if I remember this road correctly."

"The Thing?" Mellissa was curious.

"The Thing!" Kasey awoke just hearing the name.

"The Thing. Let's go there," Herbert added.

"I don't think we can afford any side trips. We've got a lot of miles ahead of us."

A roadside sign came up. On it, giant handwritten letters spelled out, The Thing.

"You're right, the Thing, it's really here," Mellissa yelled it out, excited now.

Grimsley was nothing if not a storyteller, and he had decided it was time to weave a good one, even if he made up most of it. *In this little old town on Route 66, there had been a population of only about ten people, including an old couple, Tom and Janet Prince, who ran the gas station. One late night a ghostly truck had pulled in. The station was closed, but the driver insisted on ringing the bell. Tom had finally answered, filled the guy's tank, and wiped his windshield, when the guy finally admitted he didn't have any money.*

"I've got something better than money," the stranger said.

"Unless it's gold, you better give me my gas back."

"Don't be stupid, I have something you want, something

you've always wanted, something to make you rich beyond your dreams."

"I've got pretty good dreams," Tom said.

The stranger leaned in. "I've got three bodies in the back of this truck. Don't worry, I'm not a killer; they're ancient, mummified. But if I give them to you, your life will never be the same."

It was said that Tom and Janet came around the back of the truck bed, and shined a flashlight in. Sure enough, there were three packages, and inside were the long-dehydrated carcasses of some kind of body, but within them was still the power of the undead.

"The Thing!" Mellissa called out. Another sign had come up.

"The Thing," Herbert and Kasey called out from the back.

"Une chose étrange," called out Jérôme and Fabien. Pierre even started barking.

There was two hundred miles to go between them and the famous Thing museum. Along that stretch of road are believed to be at least one hundred eighty signs featuring the Thing. Grimsley continued to embellish his made-up story, smartly telling just enough so that each person could dial up or down the horror, or the intrigue in their own mind. By the time they were up to the last five miles, even Jack was spun up.

Grimsley took out his wallet and bought tickets for everyone. Kasey and Herbert crowded around him with Pierre. He turned stern. "Nobody should go in unless they really believe they can take it."

"That was the stupidest thing I ever saw," Kasey said, as they came out the exit.

"It's too stupid to qualify as stupid. It's asinine, a tourist trap!" Herbert completed her thought.

"I think you missed the mystery, the tragedy, and the true pathos of it," Grimsley defended.

"I think the whole thing is made up," Mellissa said, taking Kasey and heading for the CLEAN RESTROOMS sign.

"*Pas de fantômes.*" Even the ghosts didn't believe any self-respecting ghost would claim those ragged dried-up mummies. They pretended to do a mummy walk, shaking their glowing parts around.

Jack looked at Grimsley. "Fake?"

"How will we ever know?"

But the Thing had done its work, as Grimsley knew it would, the ice was broken. They were all talking, arguing, complaining, bought some beef jerky and polished rocks, had a restroom stop, and the whole trip suddenly looked not just possible, but tolerable. Yes, Grimsley knew it would work, or at least he hoped it would, because it was only Grimsley who knew how difficult everything was about to become when they got to their destination.

Had any drivers on Route 66 seen them for the next few hours, they would have observed a nice red station wagon, with a badly crunched right front fender, and five people looking pretty happy driving along. Inside, it was actually seven people, just that two were no longer living, add in a dog, and despite the fact that the broken antenna had disabled the radio, they were all in song. They went through "Aquarius" and an extended version of "Let the Sunshine In," "A Boy Named Sue," and, appropriately, "It's Your Thing." This kept everyone lively for a little while, but with the deep red New Mexico sun setting, fatigue started to set in again. Grimsley opted out, resting his voice, and started sketching in his book.

Herbert dropped out and Kasey took his hand. Her other hand was trying to feel the wisps of air around Pierre's nose; they seemed lighter than normal, and the dog seemed to be getting more transparent by the hour. "I just don't know what we're going to do when we get there," Herbert said. "Am I just supposed to just let him go, and we all get back in the car?"

"You'll know what to do when we get there." Kasey tried to be positive, but she wasn't sure how she was going to react, either. But Herbert was no longer just a boy next door she was curious about or enjoyed riling up. The little dog had brought them together. They'd shared the challenges necessary to understand a mystery. It had taken both of them. What if the dog just faded away, and they didn't have another mystery to explore together?

"We just have to find ways to remember you, Pierre. Even if you are a ghost, you're the best dog anyone ever had." She scratched his hardly visible ears.

Grimsley couldn't avoid hearing them and decided to just turn around and face them. Even the normally ashen, sardonic Grimsley looked compassionate, more like their grandfather than the strange WED guy. "My whole life has been about stories. Your mother has the map, that's a story."

"Um, hello, it's just directions, there's no stories in it," Kasey corrected him, hoping he'd get his face out of their business.

"It's a collection of people's experiences; it tells

you how to find your way on this little adventure when you've never been here before."

"Have you been here before?" Herbert asked.

"I've been here many times, at a crossroads, where there's no one around, because you lost somebody. And you know you may not find them again. You don't know what's ahead of you, but you know where you've been. That's the map, and the more times you remind yourself of what that trip was, what stops and side roads you took, the more you'll remember it. Pierre, and these guys..." He gestured, sardonically at the two fading ghosts next to him. "They are maps too, maps to guide us all back here again someday." Inside, Grimsley thought he was promising too much; he checked his watch and doubted they'd get there in time. His old friends and the ghost dog would just fade away, sadly leaving them all with no stories to tell of ever having known them.

Night driving in the middle of the long trek was fatiguing, and Jack was getting to that point where he needed every trick he could think of to keep himself alert. His coffee cup was empty. He tried to talk but Mellissa was asleep. Actually, Mellissa was pretending to be asleep—she knew it was the only way to get Jack to stop talking for a little while. He nodded his head up and down and side to side. And still sleep kept

creeping out of its box and trying to overtake him. Normally, a fourteen-hundred-pound longhorn steer wandering across the road would have been something Jack noticed immediately, even stopped so that everyone could see it. But Jack's eyes were not seeing. It took a second for Mellissa's scream to wake Jack up and see his windshield filled with calico spots. She reached over, grabbed the wheel, and pulled it to the right, sliding the car onto the gravel shoulder. It spun around, until the left rear fender hit a guardrail, not so hard to be life-threatening, just enough to ensure the damage to the rear fender was a perfect match for the front. The longhorn, at least, was safely on his way. Jack stood cursing, hands in his pockets, looking at the damage. He cursed without regard to who was listening. He kicked the gravel. Then he kicked the damaged car. He rapped on the window, accusing the ghosts. "This is all your fault. We wouldn't be here if it weren't for you!"

"I think your dad's lost it." Kasey tried to hide. Herbert slid down in his seat a little and tried not to pay attention.

"Everything's fine," Mellissa said from the front seat. She knew Jack was really cursing at himself. The worst thing Jack could think of was that he could fall asleep at the wheel and endanger his family.

The crinkled station wagon pulled into a roadside restaurant, with Mellissa driving. She pulled into the very back portion of the parking lot, and everyone was happy to jump out and stretch. Jack didn't move. Mellissa walked around to his side. "Just stay here. I'll take these guys for food, and we'll bring you something." He didn't answer.

"It's okay, Jack."

The dome light faded out, and Jack looked up through the windshield into the darkness. The sky was filled with stars, he leaned back, his eyes closed, and he was soon snoring.

A bit later, there was a tussle in the parking lot. A few guys were having a disagreement, and their loud voices, along with the sound of a few bottles being tossed around, worked their way into Jack's consciousness and he shook awake. He checked the clock on the dash. *Where the heck are they?*

As Jack walked across the packed parking lot, he started to hear the noise of a raucous crowd. He came through a swinging door and the noise overwhelmed him, half asleep as he was. The saloon-style bar was packed, the tables were all full, and lots of people were standing. Many were on their chairs, waving napkins in the air. Something was happening on stage, and that had everyone oohing and aahing, in between enthusiastic cheers. He couldn't see his family anywhere. He pushed his way through the crowd until he finally reached the stage. He saw Grimsley, Kasey, and Herbert, laughing and cheering for the show. He pushed his way over to them and tried to talk but no one could hear him over the noise. He yelled to Herbert, "Where is your mother?"

Herbert laughed and pointed toward the stage. Jack

looked up and realized Mellissa was center stage, the crowd cheering at her every move. She sat on a stool behind a small table and in front of her was the largest steak Jack had ever seen. It was two inches thick and hanging over a large plate. Mellissa was rushing to eat the giant thing with a big contest clock running behind her. Each time she cut off a chunk of meat, she quickly sliced it into four pieces, and she took the smallest one. Standing right next to her, Jérôme and Fabien each reached in and consumed two other pieces, and Fabien grabbed the fourth piece, held it off the table, and Pierre leaped off the floor and grabbed it in midair like he was a jumping gator. This process continued until the steak dwindled down to a final slice. Mellissa stood up in front of the chanting crowd, turned to the side as if to show a full belly, held up the last piece, and then chewed it like she had not eaten in weeks. The clock stopped, confetti was thrown, and photographers rushed the stage and started flashing pictures.

Their dinner was free. Mellissa had just broken the previous record of eight minutes and fifty-two seconds, by a full thirty seconds. Although Jack hastily escorted them all out of the restaurant, a plaque that read MELLISSA, LAST NAME UNKNOWN would remain on the restaurant wall until nine years later, when her record would be broken by a five-hundred-pound Siberian tiger that ate the steak in ninety seconds.

At the end of a nearly nineteen-hour day of driving, Jack splurged fifteen dollars for a space in the KOA camp in Amarillo. Grimsley kicked the ghosts out and stretched across the whole backseat. Mellissa was across the front seat, snoring like a roostered-up cowhand. After he made sure Kasey was shut safely in the rear compartment, Jack stretched out on the lawn next to the parked car, with Herbert, Jérôme, and Fabien.

"That was a fun day, wasn't it?" Jack settled down and turned his head toward Herbert.

"Dad, the day was living hell. We wrecked the car, twice, almost hit a cow, and drove for eighteen hours."

"Yeah, but it was fun, wasn't it? When are you going to do that again?"

"Never, I hope."

"Seeing your mother up there on stage, all those people, and no one even suspected she was feeding most of her steak to ghosts, and a ghost dog, that was pretty funny."

Jack started to laugh. Herbert resisted for as long as he could, then he had to laugh too. Jack rolled over and wrestled around with him, taking his blanket and pillow, as they both laughed more and more hysterically. They finally settled down, looked up at the stars, and bundled up. Crickets filled in the rest.

Jérôme and Fabien were still fading, but managed to say, *"Bonne nuit."*

Herbert said, "Dad, it was fun, it's always fun. I love you." Jack was already snoring.

Jack's leftover steak sandwich and coffee refill had restored him. Bright daylight made him optimistic that the twelve-hour, twenty-minute drive through Dallas, Baton Rouge, and into New Orleans was not just doable, but downright pleasant.

By late afternoon they were nearing Beaumont, Texas, just a few miles from the border into Louisiana, and Jack was tasting victory.

Grimsley looked toward the back. Kasey was making an attempt at math homework, and Herbert sat with a worried look, Pierre panting in his lap. "Jack, are we back on a highway soon?"

"Looks like just a couple of more miles."

Grimsley was relieved to hear it, but still worried they might arrive too late.

Jack was right and soon they returned to the massive, wide, speed-efficient I-10 interstate. There had been minimal stops or delays that day, two for gas and oil, one for take-out tacos that Mellissa passed on, but Jérôme and Fabien agreed, *"Les tacos sont délicieux,"* and one to supply the whole car with a few hours of sunflower seeds, and Prickly Pear Cactus Licorice.

"What are you worried about?" Mellissa asked Jack as they were driving clear and efficient on I-10.

"I'm not worried."

"You are worried, you've kind of tuned out, and you have that little worry crinkle above your eyes."

"What crinkle?" He fiddled with his crinkled eyebrow.

"Just tell me."

"The cars."

"There's no traffic at all."

He pointed to the opposite side. "I've been counting, there's a lot more people going the opposite direction. The weather doesn't look good." He tried the radio in vain—it was all static.

Chapter 16

The Storm

By the time they saw the New Orleans city limits sign, the rain had turned into a deluge. Herbert and Kasey had seen hail before, but this was hail like none of them had ever seen, hail the size of shooter marbles, then the size of bonkers marbles, then the size of golf balls. It pounded across the car top and sounded like it would shatter the windshield. Jack pulled off slowly, barely able to see. He pulled into a deserted gas station and stopped under the metal canopy. The car was safe, and the rain on the roof canopy made a low vibrating rumble that quickly lulled them all into an afternoon catnap.

The exhaustion of two days of traveling caught up with them, and their catnap turned into full-on sleep. They slept through sunset, and well past nine o'clock. A lone car pulled up; the headlights shone through the back window. The car door opened quietly and a man in black boots stepped out. He stepped quietly and cautiously toward the wagon, shining a flashlight onto their California license plate, and into the face of Jack, who slept deeply. Mellissa woke with a shake.

"Jack, dear, wake up, wake up calmly."

Jack barely rustled. "Why, is it time already?"

"No, Jack, there's a policeman here, calmly. Sorry, he's kind of a heavy sleeper."

Jack rolled over, facing directly into the patrolman's flashlight, opened one eye, then jolted up.

"Now settle down, friend, I'm just checking on you folks." The patrolman backed off a bit and sent the flashlight over Jack's shoulder toward the rest of the passengers.

"Shut off that light!" Grimsley wasn't an easy riser, either. The patrolman saw him pushed up against the door, even though there appeared to be plenty of space in the backseat.

"And why do you have to sit so close? I can't even breathe. Can't you shove over a little bit?" Grimsley shoved the air next to him. The patrolman watched as whatever was there, to him invisible, slid over and pushed Grimsley even harder against his door.

"Is that guy okay?"

"He just likes his space." Mellissa straightened herself.

"Well, he's got the whole backseat."

The rear door was thrown open, and Pierre jumped out. Herbert jumped out and chased the dog, following him over to a tree. "Hurry up, boy!"

The officer watched Herbert chase after nothing, then he looked curiously at Jack. "What is this?"

"He's got a good imagination! But heck, no dogs, no ghost dogs anyway, no pets at all, really. Hard to travel with, we've already got a car full."

"Maybe you'd best step out a minute, just to make sure your driving is up to it tonight."

The ghosts started to rustle around, and Herbert returned to the back.

"Wipe his feet," Mellissa said, then corrected herself, "wipe your feet." She shook her head. "Kids!"

Kasey was just waking up, and a little irritable too.

"Get that dog's cold feet off of me!"

Getting impatient, Grimsley rolled down his window a crack. "Friend, if you don't have anything specific, you better just let us go. We've got a busy night ahead of us delivering some ghosts and we've got to be there before midnight, or our séance won't take, so we don't have a lot of time for your doughnut and coffee chitchat."

Pierre ran up onto Grimsley's lap, panting and putting his nose and tongue out the crack in the window. The patrolman leaned in, trying to figure out where the sound was coming from, and why he could see little bursts of condensation coming and going from Pierre's breath on the glass. The dog's paws went up on the window, leaving big muddy footprints, and then streaking the glass as he slid down. Grimsley tried an ironic smile, through the dog paw streaks.

The confused patrolman turned slowly to Jack. "Be careful, Camille's on her way. You folks better do your business and take shelter."

Jack started the engine and smiled at the patrolman. "Absolutely, sir, just dropping them all off, and then we're on our way!"

Jack gunned it and slid into motion, heading out of the station as quickly and legally as he could. He called back,

"Thank you, sir. Have a wonderful night!" Relieved, he closed his window. "What's he so nervous about? And who's Camille, anyway?"

The rain and hail continued, making it slow traveling toward the center of New Orleans. Grimsley knew the town better, so he traded seats with Mellissa to help Jack navigate. Jack still had an unsettled feeling. "Why is everything so deserted?"

"Just the rain. Everyone stayed home tonight, I guess." Grimsley read his map. "Oh, sorry, turn here!"

"Here?"

"Right here."

Jack missed the turn.

"Sorry, it came up too fast. Keep straight and I'll find another way."

With Grimsley fumbling with the map, and the rain almost blinding Jack, they became progressively lost.

Grimsley checked the clock on the dashboard—it was nearly ten o'clock. "How did we get so late? We've only got two hours left!"

"Perhaps we could stop and ask somebody for directions?" Mellissa looked out the window, hoping for a shop or gas station but nothing was open; she had a hunch neither of them would ask, anyway.

Clouded by their mutual anxiety and confusion, Grimsley and Jack managed to convince each other they were quite close to the TripTik address for the Beauregard House.

They thought they were only about a quarter mile away. If the weather was clear, they could probably have seen it.

"Yeah, I think it's just straight this way."

"I think so too." Jack drove confidently ahead.

"Stop, oh lord, help us, stop!"

As close as they were to their destination, the problem was that the last quarter of the mile was water, rushing water. Somehow, they had navigated themselves to Algiers Point, which sits right across from the French Quarter, separated by the meandering Mississippi River, and Jack was about to drive right into it. The brakes worked as well as they could in a downpour, and despite hydroplaning, Jack brought the car to a stop with the bumper just contacting an orange and white CAUTION barricade.

"That was kind a close." It was an understatement; Jack knew it was dangerously close.

Grimsley took a deep breath and looked at the clock again. "We're okay. Let's just turn around, and we'll find a bridge to go across the river."

Jack agreed, took his own deep breath, and turned the car to the left, easing it along to turn around. The car slid and felt unsteady, so Jack gave it more gas, but that slid the right side of the car around, and before Jack or Grimsley could understand what was happening, the rear wheel of the car had slipped and was just spinning, without getting any traction.

"I think you're stuck on something." Grimsley tried to see behind him, but it was too dark. "Hold on." Rain blew in as he opened the door and turned to step out. "Oh, oh!" He struggled to pull himself back in the door and slammed it shut.

"What is it, Grimsley?"

Grimsley was shaken. "We're over the river. The rear right tire is hanging over the levee!"

The entire car was leaning over to the right, and everyone quickly slid to the left, trying to keep the car in precarious balance.

"Let's just stay calm," Jack said in an obvious panic.

Grimsley was the only one who could think straight, "Jack, you need to stay on the wheel. Everyone else, stay where you are. I just need to give it a little push, and we're back on our way."

"I'll go!" Herbert started for the left door.

"Stay in this car!" Mellissa's tone was not negotiable.

"Stay in, and stay over to the left side, everybody! I'll be right back." He said it like he was just stepping out to pick a few flowers. Grimsley opened the door, a crack this time, trying to see a safe route to the back of the car.

"You need a light—take this." Jack grabbed a flashlight out of the glove box.

"That's better, thanks." Actually, it was worse. The light gave Grimsley a better view of a terrible scene. He had a narrow ledge of broken asphalt to crawl out on, and the river was high and rushing close to the top of the levee. He wasn't sure how he'd get around the right wheel, which was hanging out over the levee.

"*Attendez!*" Despite their weak state, Jérôme and Fabien were helping each other up. "*Attendez que nous venons vous aider!*"

"There's nothing they can do. They'll just be in your way," Jack held on to the steering wheel and stretched over to hold on to Grimsley's arm as he carefully stepped out.

"*Reste à l'intérieur, tu es déjà faible,*" Grimsley said carefully.

"Rest inside, you're already weak as it is." Mellissa motioned to them. They straightened, broad shouldered, proud.

"*Madame, nous pouvons t'aider, nous sommes de fiers soldats!*" Fabien spoke with determination.

Jérôme straightened his uniform and his gold epaulets and looked at them all. "*Ecoutez!*" He paused to form the words and spoke in English for the very first time. "Listen, we are proud soldiers, *les dangereux,* it is our work. We have never left a friend behind!"

Fabien repeated the cry, with a salute. "*Nous ne laisserons pas un ami!*"

Jérôme said it again. "We have never left a friend behind!"

And with that, the two ghosts passed through the car, and out onto the ledge, where they steadied Grimsley as he held the top of the car, and slid, step-by-step along the narrow levee toward the rear. He slipped a few times, but Jérôme and Fabien used whatever strength they had left to keep him from falling. When he reached the end of the car, he realized it was way out over the river. He held on to the roof rack and tried to swing his legs around, but he slipped, one arm coming down.

"He's falling!" Herbert felt helpless as he and Kasey watched Grimsley struggle against the slippery back window.

Pierre barked, mustered his energy, jumped up, and passed right through the roof of the car. Then he stretched out as much as he could, grabbed Grimsley's coat sleeve by his teeth, and pulled his arm up toward the roof rack, until finally, Grimsley caught hold of it.

Safely on the land side, Grimsley motioned to Jack from the back of the car, letting him know to be ready to hit the accelerator. He got hold of the left side of the car, and the two ghosts joined him. Pierre even got down and pushed against the bumper.

"Heave-ho," Grimsley called out.

"Heave-ho," the ghosts repeated.

Inside the car, Herbert yelled out, "They need help, I'm going."

"Young man, you stay in this…" Before Mellissa could get the words out, Herbert had opened a side door and was outside. Kasey watched anxiously through the back window.

"Heave-ho," Grimsley called out.

"Heave-ho," the ghosts and Herbert repeated.

They all gave it everything they had, and Grimsley made a rotating motion with his hands. Jack eased on the accelerator. They pushed more, and slowly in the thick mud the car began to turn. But it still wasn't enough. The rainwater was rising above their ankles, and they could barely steady themselves.

"More, a little more," Grimsley called out. They all leaned in; it was agonizing but they refused to give up.

Jack accelerated, the car spun, and the right rear tire finally grabbed hold of the levee. The car sped forward, away from the edge, and down onto the road, safe from the river.

"They did it!" Kasey called out.

Jack jumped out of the car and called out to Grimsley against the wind and pouring rain. "Grimsley, you did it!" He looked out and saw Grimsley and Herbert, standing alone in the rain. "It's all good, get back in the car!"

Grimsley put his arm around Herbert, looked back toward Jack, and called out against the storm. "They're gone, Jack, they're all gone."

The car was silent. With only mortals on board, it seemed very empty. Jack drove down the streets of the French Quarter. Everything was deserted, signs swung in the wind.

"All this way and it's no use." Mellissa looked back toward Grimsley, who had an arm around Herbert, and Kasey, who reached over from the back to put her hand on Herbert's other shoulder.

Grimsley checked his watch. "They gave it all they had; they didn't have anything left. If they could have just held on until we got here." It was eleven fifteen. "Jack, this is Toulouse Street. Turn left on Bourbon Street, go down to Dumain, and stop on the corner." Grimsley leaned down to Herbert. "I don't know if this will work, but where I come from, we say it's kind of fun to do the impossible."

"Let's try it," said Kasey.

"Are you in, Herbert?" Grimsley asked.

"I'd do anything for them."

"Okay, let's give it a try, but I'm in unknown territory here. I think I'm going to need some help." He looked out the window. "This place is cleared out, but I hope she's still there."

Without a radio, and with no one around to tell them, they had driven into the dead center of Hurricane Camille, the second-most intense tropical cyclone on record to strike the United States. The most intense storm of the 1969 Atlantic hurricane season, Camille was making landfall just as Jack was navigating the foot-high water filling Bourbon Street. As far as they could tell, they were the only people left in New Orleans, and Grimsley was hoping against hope that there was one person who didn't heed the evacuation orders.

Jack pulled up to the corner, and there was one shop with dim lights on. A tree had fallen over in front of it, and the neon sign, which said MARIE-DESTINE, MYSTIC ADVISOR, had many of its letters broken.

They all huddled under a small canopy as Grimsley rang the bell a few times. Finally, the door opened, and a woman appeared. She looked closely in disbelief. "Grimsley, is that you? The last time I saw you, you looked half-dead. Have you gone all the way over now?"

"Thank God, you're still here," Grimsley said. "Let us in."

"Let you in? It's a hurricane out there!"

"We need your help!"

"You need to get to a shelter." She slammed the door.

Grimsley knocked again. "She can be a little coarse until you get to know her." He pounded. "Open the door!"

She opened it a crack, and the chain kept Grimsley from pushing it all the way.

"I've got one can of soup and no room."

"Why didn't you evacuate?"

"I stayed because you called me. You made me miss the last bus."

"I didn't call you."

"Oh yes you did," she insisted.

"I haven't been near a phone in two days."

The wind howled, and she had to yell over it. "I didn't say you called me on the phone, but you called me."

"Then open the damn door. However I called you, we need you!"

The door swung open, they crowded in, and when the door closed, the rain stopped beating on them, and the howl of the wind was muffled. Surrounding them from all sides were votive candles, flickering and casting strange shapes on the ceiling.

"Welcome, foolish mortals," she said.

Grimsley shook some of the water and hail off his head and coat. "This is Madame Marie-Destine. She's for real, or at least she thinks she is."

Yes, she looked alive, but Herbert thought she looked like she was pretty well-connected to the other side. She was dressed in dark purple, fluorescent green fabric layers, which gave her an other-worldly glow. She spoke as if there were more souls she heard around her than were actually in the room. "Why on earth would you come here in the middle of a hurricane?"

"We didn't know it, our radio's broken," Jack explained.

"We would have come here anyway," Grimsley admitted.

"We're out of time." Melllissa looked at her, with dim hope this eccentric mystic surrounded by candles could help them at this point.

Grimsley had to work hard and fast to convince Madame Marie-Destine to make the trip up to the Beauregard

Mansion in the middle of a hurricane. He told her the whole story, everything that happened, and why this very night was so critical. She tried every excuse; her health couldn't take it; her conjuring powers weren't what they used to be; she had gout in her left foot; she had a cat; nothing worked. She sat down on a heavy, tapestry-covered sofa, folded her arms, and refused to move. But then she saw Herbert, sitting sadly on a chair, with Kasey next to him.

"Come here, young man." She beckoned him to the sofa; he reluctantly came over. He sat, then she pointed for him to move closer. She looked at him, examining his sad eyes with her aged, bloodshot ones.

"Are you a good student?"

"I am."

"What do you want to be?"

"Something with history."

"Why on earth do you like ghosts?"

"I think they like me. I'm nice to them, I think they've got a right..."

"And what right is that Herbert?"

"I don't think they deserve to just disappear. They have their stories, their battles, the ones they lost and the ones they won, people they've hated and people they've loved. We don't know that much about them, but I know they deserve to be remembered, even if it's only us that do the remembering."

"Hand me my tea," she said.

On the table in front of them lit by a burning candle was an ornamental teacup, resting on a saucer with a macramé doily. He reached for the cup.

"No, don't pick it up." She held on to both of his hands. "Just bring it to me." She locked eyes with Herbert, anticipating; they focused together. The cup didn't move. She broke away.

"Just as I thought. You don't have any special powers, or magic."

"What?" Grimsley was trying to understand.

"You have something bigger, something stronger." She moved back, locked on Herbert's eyes again.

"What's that?" Mellissa asked.

"You know what it is, Herbert."

If it was possible for her to get any closer, she did.

"You have sympathetic vibrations; do you feel them?"

"I'm not sure."

"Think about it, Herbert."

Herbert closed his eyes. He tried to think about where the ghosts were, he saw their faces, he saw Pierre panting and heard him bark. Then in his mind, the images were fading, becoming wispy circles of dust.

"They're going away."

"It's true, you do feel them, don't you Herbert?"

"I do."

Her teacup started to shake, it shook and shook, the spoon inside it rattled violently until it broke the cup, spilling all the tea out into the saucer.

The clock struck eleven-thirty, and every candle in the shop went out.

From the darkness, Madame Marie-Destine said, "Herbert?"

"Yes?"

"Let's go find your dog!"

Ghost Dog

Chapter 17

The Beauregard House

The iron gates at the driveway of the Beauregard House had rusted open, crumbled into the ground, and the grass had grown in around them. The rain had stopped, but the wind was whipping through the Spanish moss that filled the massive oak trees. The house was dark, but knocking sounds came from old wooden shutters that covered three round-arch windows, pounding in and out from the wind. A gilded weather vane on top of a cupola squeaked and turned in the wind.

The door was not locked, and it was easy for Grimsley to push it open. A lightning flash lit the foyer for a moment, revealing a massive gargoyle at the base of a staircase. Mellissa screamed and Grimsley held his heart, steadying himself. The wind slammed the front door shut.

In the darkness, Grimsley said, "There's no turning back now."

Around the foyer were the remnants of an ancient wake, a few wooden chairs, an empty coffin stand, and wilted flowers scattered around the floor. As Grimsley traced the room with the flashlight, a raven, red eyes glowing, with massive black wings, jumped up from the music stand it was perched on, flew over their heads, and disappeared out a side window.

"Pigeons," Grimsley said.

"That's some pigeon," Jack said.

They ascended the long ornamental staircase. Madame Marie-Destine took the lead, Herbert right behind, then Grimsley, Kasey, Mellissa, and Jack. Grimsley's shaky grip on the flashlight cast strange moving shadows of Madame Marie-Destine and Herbert on the ornate wallpaper. At the top of the stairs were two hallways. She looked at Herbert, and he pointed toward the left. The wind was so loud and powerful it shook everything in the house. Shattered glass came showering down on them, as the skylight in the dome above broke apart in a gust.

She led them down an impossibly long hallway. A large grandfather clock, its hands tarnished into strange contortions, ticktocked and then rang out at eleven forty-five.

She moved faster, trying to get down the hallway, but it seemed to get longer the more steps she took. Portraits and busts along the hallway were faded and had streaks across them from roof leaks, turning simple flattering likenesses into grotesque versions of their subjects. There was one candelabra at the end of the hall. It seemed to float in the mist and wind, but it lit their path to the end.

Madame Marie-Destine asked Herbert again, and he pointed to the right. She took that hall, and it quickly opened into a huge, cavernous space, the ceiling high above them, and the floor a full story below. The flashlight was almost useless in such a huge dark space. Jack stepped off the main path and went tumbling down a half flight of stairs, landing flat on the landing.

"I'm all right," he said, slowly getting up. The walls

seemed to have tiny eyes everywhere, watching his every move. "Nice wallpaper."

They descended the stairs into the cavernous space. The walls were moldy and there were huge, tarnished chandeliers. In the center of the room was a giant dining table. The flashlight frightened pigeons and rats, all of which fluttered or scurried away. The table was set, the dishes aged and cracked, silver tarnished, and linens eroded into threads of dust. Champagne bottles and glasses were woven together by cascading draperies of spiderwebs.

Madame Marie-Destine pulled out a dusty chair and sat down. "Okay, let's get to work." Within a few minutes they had formed an impromptu séance table. Chairs were dusted of spiderwebs and placed in a circle around a small serving table. An old white tablecloth dressed up the dirty wood surface.

Herbert brought over a candle lantern that had a brass art nouveau base, tarnished green by years of neglect. "Will this work?"

Madame Marie-Destine admired the lantern, struck a match, and lit it. "Perfect, Herbert," she said. "Might even help to set the mood."

The house creaked and shook, and the wind

hammered against the structure so hard, it seemed doubtful it could stay standing.

Everyone took places, and Madame Marie-Destine tried to speak as loud as she could. "All join hands!" Her frail voice strained as she tried to continue over the wind.

"When hinges creak in doorless chambers, and strange and frightening sounds echo through the halls, whenever candle lights flicker, where the air is deathly still, that is the time when ghosts are present, practicing their terror with ghoulish delight."

The wind whipped around them, debris blowing in little circles.

"Not exactly deathly still," Jack said in a loud whisper.

"Shut up," Mellissa warned him.

Thunder rumbled outside, and the room shook again, but Madame Marie-Destine no longer noticed. Her eyes were glassy, and she was deeply in a trance. The candle lantern shook, making waves of strange shadows across the room, "Herbert, do you feel ghosts with us tonight?"

"I think so. Yes, I am sure," Herbert confirmed.

"Mellissa? You feel them too, I believe," she asked.

"Why is she asking you?" Jack whispered.

"I do. Yes, I think I do," she confirmed, ignoring him.

A shiver went up Kasey's back. She held on to Herbert and Mellissa's hands and closed her eyes.

Madame Marie-Destine peeked out of one eye. She didn't seem to spy any ghosts around. "Now we move to the incantations. Each one of you will be called upon to share with the others something you deeply love about these ghosts. Get your thoughts together, there won't be much time."

The Beauregard House

Lightning flashes lit the entire ballroom, distorting normal objects into grotesque creatures.

Madame Marie-Destine continued. "Serpents and spiders, tail of a rat, call in the spirits wherever they're at..."

"Wherever they *are*, grammatically speaking," Grimsley corrected.

"It rhymes, Grimsley! Now each of you, collect your thoughts, tell me what you most remember, what you most love, and do it quick before this house falls on all of us!"

"Well, I guess I've known them the longest," Grimsley said, "and recently I've realized I have fewer years ahead than behind me. I guess it's surprising that from a couple of dead people, I learned to live life to its fullest."

"Good start, Grimsley. Jack?"

"Pass."

"Cassie?"

"Kasey."

"Close enough. Let's go!"

"They're nice." Kasey said.

"Kasey, if you believe in what we're doing, you're going to have to do better than that."

"At first, I thought it was a trick, or something had gone wrong in Herbie's head. But then the ghost dog saved my real dog. I knew we had to figure it out. We worked so hard together, day and night. And when I finally saw Pierre, with my own eyes..."

A gust of wind circulated around her, they all had to hold down the table that seemed like it might be lifted up in the wind.

Kasey went on. "When I finally saw him, I knew we did what we were meant to do, something we were destined to do, and we did it together."

Jack cleared his throat. Mellissa squeezed his hand, with love, and hoping to break a finger.

"Mellissa?"

"Great beignets."

"Mellissa?"

"Mom?"

The clock began to ring twelve, one low deep bong at a time.

"We have one minute left," Madame Marie-Destine noted.

Mellissa shook, trying to hold back tears, which finally flowed. "They brought laughter to our house for the first time in a long time," Mellissa said. "Maybe the first time ever."

"Herbert."

The wind shook the shutters above them, causing them to hammer against the walls. The clock bongs continued.

"Herbert?"

"I can't remember. I can't remember them at all."

"Herbert, you have to try."

"They're gone."

Grimsley scrambled to his bag, grabbed his sketchbook, and opened it in front of Herbert. On the page was the sketch Grimsley had done in his office, to Herbie's description. "You can remember them, Herbie, this is your memory. I only sketched it."

Herbert thought and stared at the sketch. "I remember he drank water, and you could see it pass right though him. I remember something about basketball. How my dad got all freaked the first time he saw him." Herbert laughed, but then his voice shook. "I remember...no, there's just nothing, I can't remember anymore."

The rain from the windows above came down on them and onto the table. Huge droplets hit Grimsley's sketchbook, and the image started washing away.

"Jack?" Madame Marie-Destine said.

"I don't remember anything, either."

"Jack, you have to," shouted Mellissa.

"Try, Jack," added Grimsley.

The house was being shaken apart. "Dad, try! Please try!"

"I remember one thing, just one."

"Now would be a good time, Jack," encouraged Madame Marie-Destine.

Jack tried to form the words. They came slowly, with effort. "I remember, today," he said, "on the levee."

Grimsley implored him. "Say it, Jack."

Jack struggled to form the words.

"Dad!"

Jack looked around the table, at his son, at Mellissa. "They saved my family's life."

With Jack's words, the last bong of twelve struck, and the house went completely silent, the weather outside completely peaceful.

"It stopped," Mellissa said.

"It's the eye of the storm," Grimsley said. "It's right over us."

Madame Marie-Destine looked up, and with a foreboding tone she said, "There are so many eyes upon us, countless eyes, watching us, from everywhere."

But there was nothing, no sound, no ghosts, just the group of them silently holding hands in a dark, empty, cavernous room. Herbert and Kasey tried to hold back tears, and Mellissa couldn't. Jack looked around, trying to figure out what went wrong.

"I guess we really were too late," Grimsley said. But then he jumped up suddenly and steadied himself, as Jérôme and Fabien appeared, ran toward him, jumped through him, and back again.

"Darn it, I told you never to do that!"

They gave Herbert and Kasey a huge hug, and then Mellissa. Jack stood up and tried to make a peaceful gesture of shaking their ethereal hands, a challenge just to try to hold on to them.

They all waited, but nothing else happened. Kasey put her hand on Herbert's shoulder. "I guess that's it."

Grimsley stood and walked toward the center of the silent room. "Well, I've never known a haunted mansion that couldn't muster up a swinging wake." He raised his voice to a shout, *"Que la fête commence!"*

Jérôme and Fabien joined in together. *"Que la fête commence!"*

Nothing happened.

Grimsley looked around, searching for any sign. He clapped his hands, and shouted out, *"Vite, vite!"*

And then, from every corner, from every window, ghosts came pouring in. They were dancing, they were dining, they were singing and playing instruments. There was a wedding going on, a duel, and even a huge organ being played. Conservatory doors opened as guests stepped out of carriages and came in from the garden.

And suddenly, through all the carriage wheels, and the long skirts and the draped tablecloths, came a dog. He ran through the obstacle course of people and service carts, jumped, slid across the séance table, and landed right in Herbert's lap, tongue out, slobbering, and barking his head off.

At this point, the exhausted travelers realized it was time to go home, and that meant it was time for everyone to say good-bye. Time to take the memories of the ghost dog and his friends, and everything that had happened, with them, securely, in their hearts. Grimsley patted the ghost dog, and handed him to Mellissa and Jack, who scratched him behind his ears. They handed him to Kasey, who held him close, looked into his eyes, and handed him to Herbert.

Madame Marie-Destine stood. "Herbert, are you ready?"

"Yes, I'm ready."

She led Herbert out to an edge of bright blue light, spanning the full length of the ballroom. Across the light from them was assembled a wide half-circle of ghost guests, and at the center stood Jérôme and Fabien. Herbert realized they stood on the almost invisible line of eternity, six mortals on one side, two proud ghost soldiers and all their friends on

the other, and a ghost dog in between. Herbert looked into Pierre's eyes. The dog seemed torn, comfortable in his arms, yet ready to go back to the place he belonged.

The memories of their time together were being permanently etched into Herbert's mind. Memories, it seemed, were stories after all, stories meant to be shared and cherished for all time. And whatever line divided their two worlds, it was so thin, so insubstantial, it was a scattering of stardust, or just a tiny wisp of air, barely enough to blow out a candle.

Herbert hugged Pierre for the last time, outstretched his arms, and the dog leapt through the light to the waiting arms of Jérôme and Fabien.

Ghost Dog

Chapter 18

A Little Surprise
-a few months later-

It turns out it's not that easy to recover from a road trip, especially one that involves nearly fifty hours on the road with barely a nap here and there along the way. It had been awhile and Herbert was still sleeping late. The doorbell rang, and he covered his head with his pillow.

"Herbert, it's Kasey." Mellissa tapped on his door.

"Not now." Herbert didn't want to be drawn out of his comfortable deep sleep.

A Little Surprise

"Actually, I think you probably want to come *right now*," Jack said.

The front door was partially open, morning light spilled in around it, and Herbert approached begrudgingly in his pajamas. He pushed open the door to see Kasey, looking pretty despite Herbert's sleepy half-closed eyes. Kasey held her excited poodle, Princess, back as Herbert's mom and dad were on their knees, looking at something. Herbert looked down, and at his feet was a large box of squirming puppies.

Herbert leaned down, heard the little whimpers, and smelled the combination of milk and soap.

"Want one?" Jack offered.

"One," Mellissa added. "You have to pick."

"Can I really?"

His parents' faces confirmed the approval.

Herbert had no idea how to tell which of the eight puppies might be right for him.

Kasey came down to the box and took Herbert's hand. "Just hold it out, the right one will come to you."

Herbert tried, but none of the puppies took notice. Then, the weakest-looking one, the farthest away, squirmed and tumbled out of the box, right into Herbert's hand. He held it close and brought it right up to his face. It sniffed him and licked his ear.

Kasey asked, "Is this the one?"

Herbert agreed. "This is the one."

For one brief moment—and only Herbert saw it—there was, in the puppy's eyes, a bright flash of blue lightning.

Ghost Dog

Acknowledgements

This story is a work of fiction, written with gratitude to those Disney Imagineers who created the Haunted Mansion. The attraction endures today, as powerfully as it did when it opened at Disneyland in 1969. Most especially Marc Davis and Claude Coats, X Atencio, Rolly Crump, Leota Toombs, Blaine Gibson, and Yale Gracey, many of whom I had the honor of meeting in my early days at WED Enterprises before it was later renamed Walt Disney Imagineering. I paid tribute in this story to Rolly's original idea for a Museum of the Weird, with a coffin clock and a candle man. The idea got Rolly a guest appearance on television with Walt Disney but regretfully was never finished. It exists in our collective imaginations.

Many a long night spent working late on challenging projects has been brightened for me by listening to the original recording sessions of narrator Paul Frees and X Atencio. And I cannot imagine the Haunted Mansion without their collective fun, banter, and genius.

Although I wasn't there opening day, I know I experienced the Haunted Mansion sometime in its first year. I was twelve years old and living in Southern California, a frequent visitor to Disneyland. The brilliance of all Imagineers inspired me before I knew what WED Enterprises was, and at the time I couldn't have known I'd spend nearly my entire career and much of my adult life steeped in the passion and collective imagination of the place.

I discovered books are very hard to do, and you need collaborators who believe in you. For that, I am forever grateful to The Old Mill Press. Dave Bossert saw my spark of imagination, encouraged me to keep refining it, and the book's design is thanks to the singular artistic vision and graphic genius of Nancy Bossert.

Thanks to Barbara Phillips, patient reader, editor, essential to this novice writer.

And thanks to my wonderful co-conspirator, artist George Scribner, for bringing emotion and story to every ink line, shadow and expression, for enriching, without limiting every reader's own imagination.

Walt Disney loved dogs, as I do. Canines have been key to so many Disney stories, perhaps the most famous, the key-carrying jail dog from the Pirates attraction and films. And of course, those dogs of the Haunted Mansion. I always wished that ghost dog would follow me home.

Now, thanks to all of you, he has.

Bob Weis

Pasadena, California

About the Author

Bob Weis grew up in Southern California, a frequent visitor to Disneyland.

He started his career at WED Enterprises in 1980. He spent 35 years as an Imagineer, including six years as President of Walt Disney Imagineering, and a year as Imagineering Global Ambassador.

Bob's art, storytelling, and design, and his innovative spirit have touched every Disney property around the world, including attractions, resorts, and the cruise ships, most recently the Disney Wish.

Bob is the recipient of multiple honors from the Themed Entertainment Association, including Best New Theme Park for the ten square kilometer Shanghai Disney Resort and the Buzz Price Lifetime Achievement Award. He has been awarded honorary Ph.D.s from California Polytechnic University, and from the Savannah College of Art and Design. But he is most proud to have received a Mouscar, Walt Disney's answer to the Oscar, awarded to him by Bob Iger in 2022, and the first second floor tribute window at the Disney Hollywood Studios at Walt Disney World.

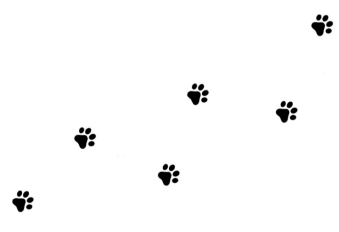

About the Illustrator

George Scribner was born and raised in the Republic of Panama, where he attended grade school and drew his way through most of his classes. He was an animator at Walt Disney Feature Animation in the mid-1980s and in 1988 he directed Oliver & Company.

He is a frequent collaborator with Walt Disney Imagineering leading creative projects with an emphasis on storytelling and animation for Disney Parks.

Scribner is also an accomplished painter who recently completed documenting the expansion of the Panama Canal through a series of paintings that capture both the magnitude of the project as well as the unique culture and stories of the people of Panama.